ALSO BY

The Trouble With Words

Little White Lies and Butterflies

The French Escape

Six Steps To Happiness

For my sister Jane
Thank you for all your support, for cheering me on and most of all, for keeping me sane.
Your words of wisdom and thumbs up selfies will be forever remembered.

1

EIGHT DAYS UNTIL CHRISTMAS

"What do you think?" I held a yellow, sleeveless shift dress against my body. It had hung in my wardrobe for months; an impulse buy that I still wasn't sure my legs could carry off. I'd bought it after catching sight of myself in a shop mirror and realising I looked more like a fifteen-year-old Rebel Wilson than the grown woman I was meant to be.

I decided there and then that I needed an overhaul and grabbed the first colourful item of clothing to hand. Hence, the yellow dress. I frowned. Despite any good intentions, that was as far as any supposed change went.

Standing there in my bedroom looking at myself once more, I wished I'd seen that revamp through. With less than a week until my holiday, I looked no different in that moment than I had back in the summer. I sighed, considering whether the dress really merited packing space, before turning to my sister for her opinion. "What do you think, Vee?" I asked.

Out of the two of us, I'd always been the geek, preferring to lose myself in a good book as opposed to some glossy fashion magazine. I tended to live in jeans, T-shirts and pumps, and while my overgrown mop of hair was treated to the odd cut, it had never so much as had a hint of colour near it. I was the same when it came to make-up. Apart from a touch of mascara and lip gloss, I didn't really bother. Unless I was on a night out. Then I jazzed things up with a stroke of eyeliner.

Vee, on the other hand, had always been a fashionista. Even at eight months pregnant she could have been a model. She was lucky to have inherited Mum's tall, *eat all you want, you won't gain an ounce* physique. It was no wonder Vee made the perfect clothes horse. Unlike me, who took after our father. I looked down at the dress once more telling myself I wasn't fat, I was big-boned. "Yes or no?" I asked my sister.

Vee sat on the bed next to my suitcase, busy tidying its contents to make room for the handful of books I hoped to squeeze in. It was clear she hadn't heard me, that her mind was elsewhere. Baby brain, my brother-in-law called it, something to do with lower concentration levels in expectant mothers, which, of course, Mitch would know all about. The man seemed to have devoured every pregnancy book on the market and I wouldn't have been surprised if he were prepping to deliver the baby himself. When it came to his wife's gestation Mitch was a walking, talking encyclopaedia, with no qualms about sharing his knowledge with the rest of us. When listening to him, I might have admired his dedication, but the number of times my eyes had glazed over made me wonder if baby brain was catching.

"Vee?" I said, wanting to get on with the task at hand.

Finally, she looked up. "Ooh, yes," she said, nodding as I indicated the dress. "That colour's perfect with a tan."

I wrinkled my nose, still not keen. "You don't think it's too short for knees like these?"

Vee glanced at my patella and rolled her eyes. "No, Holly. It's fine."

Although not convinced, I still passed it over, preferring to focus on the bronzed glow that Vee mentioned. I saw myself applying sun cream and catching rays as I lay on a sun-drenched beach; and pictured myself swimming in a vast expanse of glistening blue sea. I couldn't wait to shed my woolly jumpers and cardigans, don my swimsuit, and charge towards the water's edge ready to dive straight in. Almost able to feel the sunshine on my skin, I knew that time away from Britain's damp, cold winter weather was just what my body and soul needed. I was about to enjoy a Christmas to remember. The countdown was on.

While Vee folded the dress and put it in the case, I reached into the wardrobe once more. "And this?" I grinned as I pulled out a maxi navy-blue boat neck. Not only was it beautiful, unlike the yellow number, it was the perfect length for hiding stocky knees. It was also my *pièce de résistance*, which I intended on saving for the last evening of my trip. Just because I had to start my holiday looking like an ugly duckling didn't mean I couldn't end it as a swan.

Not usually one for clothes, as soon as I'd seen that navy-blue dress, I knew I had to have it. And after ten days of rest, recuperation, and self-reflection, wearing that dress would be symbolic. Transformation complete, it represented out with the old, and in with the new.

My sister's whole demeanour sprang to life, as she took in the smooth silky fabric. "Wow!" she said. "That would look fabulous with a pair of flat sandals." She held out her hands to take it. "It's gorgeous."

"Isn't it?" I replied. "It's the one thing I bought especially, although I shouldn't have. It cost a fortune, which, no doubt, means a few less cocktails while I'm away."

"Oh, the sacrifice."

"I know." I put the back of my hand against my forehead, feigning despair as I looked to the ceiling. "How will I cope?" I paused, waiting for Vee to chuckle at my attempt at melodrama. But instead of finding it amusing, she fell quiet, leaving me stood there like an unappreciated thespian. Wondering why the silence, I diverted my gaze to see Vee's face crumple. "What is it?" I asked. Dropping my hand, my smile vanished. "You're not in any pain, are you?"

My pulse quickened at Vee's failure to respond and feeling panicky, I told myself the dress wasn't that exciting, her contractions couldn't have started. With me about to head off on holiday, Christmas around the corner, and the baby not due for another month, the last thing anyone needed was Vee going into labour. I watched her inhale, clearly trying to compose herself, but her action did nothing to ease my racing mind. As much as I looked forward to becoming an aunty, if things were moving on that front, I had no desire to play midwife. I, too, took a deep breath and thanking goodness I knew a man who did, grabbed my phone off the dressing table. "I'll ring Mitch?"

"No!" Vee said, putting a hand up to stop me. "There's no need. I'm fine."

I froze, my thumb hovering over the screen. "Really? Because you don't look it."

"Honestly. It's not the baby."

"Then what is it?" I asked, my nerves frazzled.

"Nothing," Vee said. "I'm just being soft." She rubbed her belly. "I mean, look at me. I'm obese." She indicated the navy boat neck. "I don't think I'll ever wear a dress like this again."

I stared at my sister, unable to believe she almost gave me a heart attack over a bit of fabric. But taking in Vee's pitiful demeanour, I couldn't bring myself to tell her that. The last thing I wanted was to cause any more upset, or worse still, set off her contractions for real. And I most certainly didn't want to be a hypocrite. I thought back to the occasions when Vee had supported me through the odd wardrobe meltdown, and it wasn't as if I'd ever had pregnancy as an excuse. Sympathy enveloped me and tossing my phone on the bed, I sat down next to her. "Vee, you're four weeks away from giving birth."

"Doesn't stop me wishing I wasn't the size of a house, though, does it?"

I couldn't help but smile. The size of any kind of building my sister was not.

"It's not funny, Holly." Vee let out a mournful sigh as she looked down at her bump. "I'm beginning to wonder what's in there. An elephant? I'm surprised Mitch can bear to look at me, I can hardly look at myself these days."

It was strange to hear Vee talk like that. My sister might have always had a figure to die for, but she never paid it any attention, good or bad; it was me, with my fuller figure, who did all the complaining. Plus, everyone knew Vee's husband adored her. Forget her belly, my sister could've grown a humongous second head and Mitch would have still loved her.

Looking at her, I wanted to believe it was her hormones talking. According to *Doctor* Mitch these fluctuated during a woman's third trimester. Apparently, as her body prepared for birth mood swings were to be expected. But her comments felt too out of character for Vee and I found myself wondering if my latest relationship disaster was, at least in part, to blame for her distress. "This isn't because of what happened with you know who, is it?" I asked. "Because Mitch isn't like Jeremy."

Pictures of the last time I saw Jeremy flooded my mind. Him and some bint, both butt-naked on *my* bed. I still couldn't believe the two-timing so-and-so hadn't taken her to his own house, whether he still lived with his mother or not. Shuddering, I shook the memory away as best as I could. I'd needed a new mattress anyway; and Jeremy and his bit-on-the side had taken up too much of my headspace already.

I reached out to Vee with a comforting hand. "Mitch would never... You do know that, don't you?" Not sure who needed the reassurance more, me or my sister, I hated to think my track record in men had, in some warped, prenatal way, affected Vee's confidence.

She lifted her gaze to look at me, outrage written all over her face.

With Vee's disposition changing from one second to the next, I realised my brother-in-law might have had a point on the mood swing front and for my sake as much as my sister's, I slid my palm back to safety and shifted away from her slightly. "Good," I said, with no choice but to let the matter drop.

She turned her attention back to the suitcase.

"Because you and Mitch are like Mum and Dad. In it for the long haul."

She gave me another look. "I thought you were trying to cheer me up?"

I pictured our parents out and about, loud and proud in their matching outfits, realising that might not have been the most comforting comparison to make. For either of us, being likened to Mum and Dad was a fate too disturbing to contemplate. While the rest of the world seemed to consider our parents harmless yet eccentric, to my sister and I they were plain and simple barking. Then again, I often wondered if we all were. When it came to my family, there was never a dull moment between us.

Vee remained unamused and I couldn't help but think there was more going on in that head of hers, that there was something she wasn't telling me. "Anything you want to talk about?" I asked, making sure to keep my voice light.

"What do you mean?" she said, dismissive. "Like what?"

As much as she tried to hide it, I could see I'd touched a nerve, but, again, I didn't push. Instead, I stood up and taking my sister's hands, hoisted her onto her feet. "Come on."

"Where are we going?" she asked.

"For a cup of tea." I nodded to the packing. "That can wait. We'll do it later."

2

I stood at the front door waving Vee off as she drove away. It was going dark by then and the whole village looked magical. Brightly lit Christmas trees shone in the windows of neighbouring cottages, twinkling fairy lights wove through gardens, and an assortment of jovial plastic Santas and wicker scarf-wearing reindeers sat at gates ready to greet visitors. What with going away, I hadn't seen the point in glad-ragging my own house and as I turned to go back inside, I smiled at the comparison. There was no denying mine looked positively *bah humbug!* as a result.

I had a spring in my step as I made my way down the hall to the kitchen. Not only had I survived my sister's little meltdown and soothed her back to her usual placid self, I only had a few more days at work to get through, before jetting off to spend Christmas in the sun. I couldn't wait.

A picture of Mum and Dad popped into my head. Guilt, I realised, for *abandoning* them during the festive period, something no family member had ever dared do before. It was a choice that would, without doubt, go down in the annals of Noelle family history, but I refused to let that ruin my excitement. As a woman who'd never put a foot outside of Europe, I looked forward to venturing further afield. Not even my parents could have stopped me ending that year with a bang.

I thought back to the first time I realised my parents weren't quite like everyone else's and while they'd proven themselves to be quirkier than most many times since, it was during a primary school nativity that their uniqueness first hit home. Vee played the angel on account of her being angelic; while I had the role of guiding star for being less so. Unlike Vee, I didn't have a speaking part. Wearing a gold four-pointed tabard, with a matching pointy hat to complete my star shape, all I had to do was stand on a huge box at the back of the stage and enjoy proceedings. Apart from the bit where Balthazar, one of the three wise men, forgot his lines, everything seemed to go to plan.

That was until the headmistress took her seat at the piano and commenced the intro to *Away in a Manger*, one of my parents' all-time favourite Christmas songs. It appeared Mum and Dad weren't content to simply listen to me and the cast do the singing as outlined in the script and much to my bewilderment they rose to their feet ready to join in. Their action caused some confusion amongst the rest of the audience, although Dad waved his arms around encouraging all the other parents to join in and it wasn't long before they all stood up too.

Mum and Dad's voices rang out far above everyone else's and it soon became clear they were singing a completely different rendition to the one being played by the headmistress. My parents seemed to have gone for a more classical version. Their harmonising and operatic tones didn't just attract attention; they put everyone else in the room off their vocal stride. Fellow nativity cast members started to giggle. And there was no denying the look of frustration that crossed the headmistress's face as she sped up on the piano keys. Unfortunately, the whole song turned into a hot discordant mess until the very last note and the only people who didn't seem to notice the musical fracas were Mum and Dad.

I shook my head, dismissing the recollection as I entered the kitchen, supposing I should think about dinner. Although there wasn't much to consider. There'd been no point doing a proper shop when I wouldn't be around to eat most of it. Opening the fridge, however, I sighed in disappointment. Things were worse than I'd thought. The shelves were bare apart from a microwave curry, eggs, cheese, and half a bag of spinach.

I picked up the ready meal and stared at the image on its packaging – chunks of melt-in-the-mouth chicken, smothered in a rich, creamy masala sauce. My belly grumbled, but more in protest than hunger, as if it knew the photograph breached the Trade Descriptions Act as the meal's contents would resemble nothing of the sort. "Pizza it is," I said, swinging the fridge door shut.

I took my phone from the kitchen counter, ready to ring my order through, but before I got the chance it sounded, and Mum's name appeared on the screen. I didn't have to guess the conversation ahead; I knew what was coming. No matter how many times I told Mum I wouldn't be cancelling my holiday and that she was wasting her time thinking otherwise, the woman refused to hear a word of it. I took a deep breath in readiness. "Mum," I said, fixing a smile on my face as I answered her call. "To what do I owe the honour?"

"Are you sure you're doing the right thing?" Mum asked.

I looked up to the ceiling hoping for divine intervention. Nothing too serious; I didn't want the woman hit by a bolt of lightning. A sore throat would have done, as long as it prevented Mum from using her vocal cords. "Lovely to speak to you too," I replied.

"Because there's no shame in changing your mind."

Mum had had nine months' notice in which to get her head

around the fact that I wouldn't be around for Christmas yet had spent the entire period doing anything but. I despaired. "I haven't changed my mind, Mum."

"Well I think you should. You know how much me and your Dad..."

While Mum chunnered, I let my mind drift back to that lazy Sunday afternoon when Jeremy announced he'd organised our holiday of a lifetime.

The fire glowed orange and I lounged on the sofa, a glass of wine in one hand and a good book in the other. I may have been reading a psychological suspense novel, but I couldn't have felt more relaxed.

"I've been thinking," Jeremy said, entering the room. "About next Christmas."

"Really," I replied. As far as I was concerned, it was only March and we still hadn't recovered from the last one. "It's a bit early for that, isn't it?"

"I'm being serious," he said.

So was I.

"I've decided we should do something different this year."

I looked up from my page, his assertiveness surprising me. Jeremy had always been more of a negotiator. I'd been caught out quite a few times by his ability to make me think something was for my benefit when in reality it had been more for his. "Dangerous talk."

I knew Jeremy hadn't appreciated spending our first Christmas Day together at my parents' and that given the chance, he would have come up with any excuse to get out of going. But celebrating with Mum and Dad was a given in my family and apart from the odd gripe, he'd suffered in silence. I supposed he was bound to make a stand over our second Christmas at some point and deciding it only fair I listen, I let my book fall and swung my legs forward to make room for him to sit.

"Don't you think it would be nice to have our own little event?" he asked, plonking himself down next to me. "Just you and me, without all the fuss?"

I'd have been lying if I'd said the thought hadn't crossed my mind. But going to Mum and Dad's house wasn't just tradition, it was expected. "Yes, but..." I could already envisage their disappointment at not having us there. "You know how much they love Christmas."

"Really?" He feigned surprise.

I laughed. "Don't be like that."

He shifted round to face me. "Be honest. Where would you rather be? Here in the cold? Or somewhere hot, strolling hand in hand along stretches of white sandy beach?"

Picturing the scene, it was a far cry from all the festive sleet and slush I was used to. "I think we both know the answer to that."

"Would you rather we were shading ourselves under a palm, or gathered around a Christmas tree?"

I let out a wistful sigh. "Shading under a palm any day of the week."

Jeremy smiled. "Then how does ten days in the sun sound?"

"Heavenly." Thanks to Jeremy's word painting, I was already there.

"Worth missing out on Christmas pudding with your parents for?" he asked.

I scoffed. As romantic as he'd made it sound, Jeremy had never gone in for that kind of ardour. In the six months we'd known each other, the word *romance* hadn't featured in the man's vocabulary, let alone put that kind of pressure on his wallet. His idea of extravagance had been a bunch of garage carnations. "As if," I said.

He raised an eyebrow in response, enough to tell me he knew something I didn't. "What's really going on here?" I asked. In my experience, men only went all out when they'd been up to no good and I looked at him, suspicious. "What have you done?"

"I haven't *done* anything," Jeremy replied.

He reached into his pocket. "Unless you include this." He pulled out a folded sheet of paper and held it out.

"What is it?" I asked. Opening it up, I scanned its contents, my eyes widening in disbelief with every word. I looked from the sheet to Jeremy, telling myself that he didn't do things like book holidays. April Fools' Day had to have come early. "This is some kind of joke, right?"

"Nope, it's for real," Jeremy replied, sitting there with a big satisfied grin. He nodded to the paper in my hands. "And that's the booking confirmation to prove it."

My excitement was building. "The Caribbean? Really?"

"Really."

I giggled as I looked at the sheet again, bouncing up and down in delight. I threw my arms around Jeremy and planted a kiss on his lips, any concern for Mum and Dad disappearing into the ether.

"Are you even listening to me?" Mum said, breaking into my thoughts.

"Yes," I replied. "I'm listening."

At first, Mum did well at pretending she was okay with our plans. But the closer our holiday got, the harder it was for her to keep up the façade. Subtle hints about the importance of family time began creeping into her conversations. Then Jeremy's affair came to light, leaving me no choice but to dump the man, which opened the door for Mum's comments to become less refined. I rolled my eyes. Despite my insistence to the contrary, she seemed to have convinced herself that if she pushed hard enough, I'd stop being silly and jump back into the festive fold.

"It'll feel strange," Mum said, clearly hell-bent on keeping up the pressure.

I looked up to the heavens once more, telling myself that God loved a trier, even if I didn't. "What will?"

Her responding sigh seemed to go on forever. "Being on your own at Christmas?"

I couldn't help but smile as I envisaged our usual festivities. Waiting for us to arrive, Mum and Dad would be at the window like a couple of excited children, waving us in.

After losing ourselves under mountains of wrapping paper, they'd insist we spent the afternoon stuffing our bellies as much as humanly possible, *eat, drink and be merry* having long been the Noelle family Christmas motto. We'd watch Christmas movies and play board games. My heart warmed as I pictured Mum and Dad's happiness at having us all there. "It'll certainly be different," I replied, my heart not warming quite enough.

"For us as much as for you," Mum said, obviously going for the sympathy vote.

I forced myself not to laugh, knowing full well Mum was doing her best to hide her irritation at me not changing my mind. But whereas my sister had inherited Mum's slimline physique, her stubbornness had been passed down to me. And as much as Mum refused to accept defeat on the issue of my holiday, so did I. Short of Vee going into labour, I was getting on that plane.

"Are you sure you're doing the right thing?" she asked. "Because if something happens the last thing you want is to be stuck all that way away, with no means of getting back."

I could think of worse places to be stranded.

I knew Mum meant well, but that was the thing, a bit of me-time was just what I needed. After what Jeremy put me through, it was what I deserved. And like I said to him when he also suggested I might want to bow out, no way was my holiday going to him and his bint, and neither was it going to waste.

"Mum, it's a hotel. I'll be surrounded by people."

The line fell silent for a moment, and I could've sworn I heard the woman's cogs turning as she tried to come up with another excuse as to why I should stay at home.

"Well you won't get a proper Christmas lunch," she said. "One with all the trimmings. And *Jingle Bells* won't sound the same on a steel drum, you know."

"I'll live."

"Of course, the weirdest thing will be the weather. It'll be hot."

It was all I could do not to laugh. Winters in the Yorkshire Dales weren't exactly fun for someone like me who felt the cold. "Lots of sun, sea and sand, you mean?"

"Exactly."

"Instead of black ice and snow?" I knew I shouldn't tease, but the more Mum tried to put me off going, the more reasons she gave telling me I should.

"Oh, you know what I mean." Her voice bristled as her frustration finally came to the fore. "Joe, you talk to her," she said, calling for backup. "For the love of all that is holy, that daughter of yours won't listen to me."

Poor Dad, I thought as I waited for him to come on the line. When it came to his wife and daughters, he always seemed to be stuck in the middle.

3

"Hello, love," Dad said, while my mother grumbled in the background.

"Hi, Dad. How are you?" Knowing we were staying on the subject of my holiday, I decided to organise my flight boarding passes while we chatted and keeping the phone to my ear, I wandered through to the lounge. One handed, I grabbed my laptop, passport, and holiday booking confirmation off the sideboard and eager to get started, I took a seat on the sofa.

"I hope you weren't giving your mum a hard time just then," Dad said.

I switched on the computer and waited for it to fire up.

"She doesn't mean any harm. She just worries about you."

"I know," I replied, even though in my view the woman had nothing to worry about.

"She just wants you here, where she can keep an eye on you."

I scoffed. "Why? To make sure I'm eating properly? Getting my five-a-day?"

"Something like that." I heard the smile in Dad's voice.

The laptop sprang to life and I put Dad on loudspeaker,

before placing my phone down on the coffee table. I clicked on the internet icon, excited to check-in for my flight.

"Although I have to say," Dad said, falling serious again. "She's not the only one with concerns. You've been through a lot, thanks to *you know who*."

As I keyed the airline's name into the search bar, my heart melted a little at Dad's words. Ever since I'd caught Jeremy in flagrante delicto poor Dad hadn't been able to bring himself to say Jeremy's name. "I get that," I said. "But you both need to realise I'm a big girl and it's not as if we can't video call while I'm away. I'll even send Mum pictures of my meals if it helps."

"Is she starting to see sense?" Mum called out.

Dad chuckled. "I think it'll take more than a few snapshots, love."

Didn't I know it.

"To be honest, Holly, I was looking forward to this year's celebrations as much as your mother."

I smiled as I smoothed out the booking confirmation and opened my passport in readiness. With Mum's concerted efforts failing to have an effect, my parents had obviously decided on a two-pronged approach. "What's new? The pair of you always look forward to Christmas."

"Just the five of us," Dad said, wistful, clearly ignoring my bon mot. "You, me, Mum, Vee and Mitch."

I shook my head. The way Dad talked anyone would've thought Jeremy had been attending theirs for decades, when everyone concerned knew he'd only been the once.

The airline's home page appeared on screen. Pictures of sunny destinations, holiday ads, and price drops leapt out at me. It was thrilling to think that after a few clicks and a printout, I'd be booked on the plane ready to head off to the Caribbean, proof that I would soon be the intrepid traveller I'd spent months looking forward to becoming.

"I hope you're not offended when I say this, but *you know who* did put a dampener on things," Dad continued.

Narrowing my eyes, I scanned the screen trying to figure out what action came next.

"Sitting there with his nose in the air," Dad carried on. "As if he thought he was too good for the likes of us."

Dad was right. Jeremy might not have said anything, but he had been a bit snooty. Then again, although I'd never admit such a thing to Mum and Dad, I could appreciate why he hadn't been able to completely relax around my parents. As awful as it was to think, Mum and Dad didn't always do themselves any favours in the way they presented themselves to other people. They could be a bit full-on and while their madcap behaviour had been a cross Vee and I had had to bear from the day we were old enough to know better, it was going to take someone special to accept Mum and Dad for who they were. A someone special I'd yet to meet.

"I'm sorry, Dad. It's not that I don't want to spend Christmas with you all," I replied. I finally spotted the *Manage My Booking* button and clicked. "I just need some time to myself. To have some fun. And while I'm at it, think about what I want out of life, without work and a comfortable routine getting in the way."

"What are you talking about, what you want out of life? You have a good job, a new car, your own little house."

"Which might have been enough if I'd found someone decent to share it with." As the next web page appeared, I thought about Mum and Dad, and Vee and Mitch, envious of their relationships. Try as I might, I'd never come close to meeting *the one*. I had serious doubts I ever would.

"Just remember," Dad said, as if reading my mind. "When it comes to being part of a couple, the grass isn't always greener."

I almost laughed as I picked up the booking confirmation

and began inputting the required reference number. Like that was a lesson I hadn't already learned.

"You have your independence which, believe me, is something to be celebrated."

"Easy for you to say," I replied. "You're not the one stuck on your own."

"That's as maybe. But there are lots of people out there who envy you your position. Being able to do what you want when you want. Only yourself to think about. We lifers can get desperate for that kind of freedom at times."

"I can hear you," Mum shouted from somewhere in the background.

"See what I mean?" Dad said. "She's got eyes and ears everywhere that one."

As I finished typing in the last character, I had to admit Dad's words resonated. In my experience relationships were hard work and while Jeremy was just one in a list of idiot boyfriends, he'd proved to be the worst. My whole life seemed to revolve around him. In the fifteen months we were together there'd been a whole lot of giving on my part and a whole lot of taking on his, something I hadn't fully realised while we were a couple.

Jeremy had spent almost all his time at my place, but it wasn't as if he'd contributed in any way. I had done all the cooking, cleaning, and bill paying, on account of Jeremy not wanting "to take away my feminist rights". Although more fool me for letting him get away with it. The only thing he did do of his own free will was book a holiday and as romantic as he'd made that holiday sound, it turned out to be nothing more than a gesture of guilt because of his affair.

"You're right, Dad. Life is definitely easier as a singleton." I sighed, thinking about the energy I'd wasted on Jeremy. "That's why this holiday is so important. It's time I had some fun, some excitement. I need a new direction."

"What about getting on with that book you've always wanted to write?"

It was just like Dad to remind me of that. I'd talked about becoming an author ever since I'd learnt to read. To transport a reader into another world; to enable them to experience a journey they might never go on in real life; go to a place they might never visit. My love of the written word was the very reason I'd studied creative writing at university. Then the reality of student debt came into play and I ended up doing the next best thing – working in a bookshop. As real life took over, dreams of being a writer faded into the background. I'd been a bookseller ever since. "Exactly!" I said. "And to write I have to live. This holiday is just the beginning, Dad. Who knows where I'll be in twelve months' time?"

Dad let out a laugh, while I imagined myself shading under an umbrella on a Caribbean beach, scribbling in some fancy notebook, jotting ideas down for my magnum opus. I clicked enter on the computer screen, my excitement only increasing as I got ready to add my passport details.

My stomach lurched as a message popped up.

Booking cancelled I read.

That can't be right.

"I understand," Dad said, as if finally resigned to the fact that I wouldn't be around for Christmas. Dad lowered his voice. "Even if your Mum doesn't."

"I can still hear you," my mother said, yet again proving she had the aural equivalent of twenty-twenty vision.

"Thanks, Dad." By then I was only half listening, but even with my attention elsewhere, it was still good to know at least one of my parents finally accepted my decision.

I shrugged, telling myself I must have missed a digit some-where and needed to try again. "Sorry, Dad, but I've got to go," I said. Staring at the screen, I wanted to focus on the task at hand.

"Okay, love. Well you take care."

"Tell Mum I'll try and ring before I leave, yeah? If not, it'll be when I get to the resort, so you know I've landed and got to the hotel in one piece."

"Will do."

"Love you, Dad."

"Love you too, Holly."

I ended the call to the sound of Mum protesting that he couldn't hang up yet because he hadn't got me to change my mind. I felt sorry for leaving him to take Mum's flack on my behalf and made a mental note to bring him back something extra special from my travels.

I put all thoughts of my parents to one side, instead concentrating on every individual character as I inputted the booking reference for a second time. I paused before pressing enter, keeping everything crossed that on that occasion I'd get through to the next stage.

Booking cancelled it said again.

Confused, I tried to absorb the words in front of me, and adamant that there had to be a blip in the system, I tried again.

Booking cancelled.

A picture of Jeremy popped into my head and my heart sank. As realisation dawned, anger began to well. "How could you?" I said. "You... You... Bastard!"

I slammed the laptop lid down, at the same time asking myself how I could have been so naïve? I'd known Jeremy had the right to cancel, of course; he was the one who'd booked and paid for our trip. But that didn't stop me feeling furious. I'd assumed after what he'd done, even he wouldn't have stooped so low as to want his money back. Especially when I'd told him I had every intention of still going.

How could you be so stupid? I asked of myself.

4

I sat there dazed, trying and failing to figure out what to do. Not only was my Christmas ruined, that holiday had represented more than an escape to the sun. It was meant to herald a new way forward, the start of a brand-new outlook.

Thanks to Jeremy, who had held all the cards when it came to my trip, I felt powerless. And stuck, I realised. My bank balance wouldn't stretch to a few days in Blackpool, let alone somewhere as exotic as the Caribbean. In fact, the only Christmas I could afford was the one I'd spent the last nine months insisting I wouldn't be partaking in. "Mum's going to love this," I said.

I jumped when my phone rang to break the silence. Picking it up off the coffee table, I saw my friend's name appear on the screen. Tempted to ignore the call and instead host a pity party, I asked myself what would've been the point in that? Not speaking to people didn't change anything and it wasn't Annie's fault my ex was a conniving douche. I hit the answer button.

"Seriously," Annie said, before I could even speak. "I know she's my daughter and I love her to bits, but if I don't get out of here, I'm going to kill her."

My friend was forever complaining about her one and only offspring. Although most of the time, I appreciated why. The girl did have a penchant for drama. "Can't you just send her home?" I asked, knowing that's what I'd have done in Annie's shoes.

My cancelled holiday continued to nag at me.

Annie whimpered. "That's the problem. According to Emma, she is home."

"You mean she's back?" I asked, the uncharitable part of me relieved to know I wasn't the only one with problems. "So soon?" It didn't seem two minutes since she'd left.

Annie despaired. "Oh, she's back all right."

"Oh dear." Despite my own dilemma, I sympathised. Since her daughter moved out, Annie hadn't just grown accustomed to having her own space, she'd enjoyed the new sense of calm that came with it. Her home had gone from never having a dull moment, to it becoming her own little sanctuary.

"You can say that again," Annie replied. "She landed this afternoon, suitcase in hand." She scoffed. "Tell me again why I didn't change the locks while I had the chance."

"Poor Josh," I said, thinking of Emma's boyfriend. "He must be devastated."

"Never mind poor Josh. What about me?"

I smiled, knowing my friend didn't mean that. Annie had always been one of life's carers. If someone was celebrating, she'd celebrate with them. If someone was upset, she'd be upset for them. And if someone needed help, she'd go all-out to assist.

"No, that's not fair," she said, proving my point. "The poor lad's as distressed as I am. But that's what you get when you try to do something nice for my daughter."

When it came to Emma, I wasn't surprised to hear that whatever Josh had done, his efforts had backfired. With Emma's track record, the words *mountain* and *molehill* sprang to mind. She had a talent for creating a palaver over nothing. Not that I'd ever said that out loud. Out of respect for Annie, it was a view I'd kept to myself.

Annie let out a long drawn-out sigh. "As if I don't have enough to think about right now, she goes and does this to me. And I was so looking forward to Christmas at her house," she said.

I stared at my laptop, still reeling over my cancelled holiday. "I was looking forward to Christmas too," I replied.

Annie chuckled. "You sound as miserable as I do?"

I hadn't meant to moan. Annie clearly had enough problems with Emma, without me dumping on her as well. "Not at all," I said, trying to sound perkier. "It's nothing I can't figure out."

"Why don't I believe you?" she asked.

Annie always did know me well. "I'm sorry, Annie," I said, realising there was no point pretending. "I'm just feeling sorry for myself."

"Why? What's wrong?"

I sighed. Images of white sandy beaches, deep blue seas, and golden sunshine flitted through my head. I saw balmy evenings where I sipped cocktails from coconut shells, the blissful rhythm of calypso music playing in the background. I thought about my packed suitcase, zipped up and airport-ready. "I'm not going to the Caribbean. Jeremy cancelled the whole thing."

"You're joking." Annie's voice oozed compassion. "Oh, Holly, I'm so sorry."

"Not as sorry as I am," I said. "He didn't even have the grace to tell me."

"The bastard! And there's me wittering on about my daughter."

"Don't be daft." I recalled all the support Annie had given after Jeremy's departure. "You've listened to me talk about my problems enough times."

"So, we're both up shit creek then?" Annie said, as if resigned.

"What do you mean?" I asked, wondering if there was more going on than she'd said.

"That you're not the only one with man troubles. It's not just Emma's living arrangements that are concerning me."

"Since when?" I said. That was news to me. I'd known Annie for years and never seen her as much as look at a chap.

"Don't get too excited. It's not what you think," she said, as if reading my mind. "As I still need to get away from that daughter of mine, why don't I tell you when I see you? Pub? Half an hour?"

Usually, I'd have jumped at the chance of a night on the town but needing to figure out what to do about Christmas I wasn't convinced that was the best way to get my head around things.

"I'll give you my shoulder to cry on, if you give me yours?" Annie said, in response to my silence.

I chuckled, supposing it was either that or stay home and unpack my suitcase. "I guess a couple of hours sharing our woes might help," I said.

Annie let out a laugh. "In my case, there's no *might* about it."

I smiled, telling myself I could eat while I was out. "Okay. Make it forty-five minutes," I replied. "And you're on."

5

"Never again."

If I had a pound for every time I'd said that, I'd be a very rich woman. Not that I could work out how rich, thanks to the raging hangover beating a drum in my skull. Lamenting how much it hurt, I put a hand up to my head and felt something stuck in my hair. Pulling it free, I stared at a piece of tinsel, its silvery fronds mocking me.

Tossing it to one side, I flipped the duvet back, hauled myself out of bed and threw on my dressing gown. Making my way to the bathroom, I avoided looking in the mirror as I stood at the sink and turned on the cold tap. The morning after the night before was never pretty in my experience and deeming myself to be in enough pain, I didn't see the point in damaging my eyes too. I stuck my dry mouth under the flowing water, quenching my alcohol-induced thirst with gulp after gulp until I struggled to breathe and drink at the same time. Straightening myself up, I wiped my mouth with the back of one hand, while slamming the tap off with the other. "What were you thinking?" Yet more words that could have increased my bank balance.

Going downstairs to the kitchen, I went straight to the coffee machine. Short of a head replacement, I knew if anything was going to sort me out, it was a strong dose of caffeine. As I set about making my coffee, I asked, *Why, oh why, did I do it to myself?* Before my thoughts turned to the previous evening.

The pub had been packed thanks to a works Christmas party and as was usual when it came to these things, people revelled in boisterous excitement.

"Merry Christmas!" people shouted over the music.

"Ho! Ho! Ho!" others replied.

High-spirited conversations, Rudolph reindeer sweaters, and Santa hats abounded. It seemed everyone looked forward to a bit of downtime and merriment. At least, everyone except me and Annie.

Making our way through the crowd, we secreted ourselves in a corner away from the hullaballoo. We wore no sign of yuletide gaiety and while such a fun-filled atmosphere might not have been conducive to two women in need of drowning their sorrows, drown our sorrows we did.

"I can't believe my holiday's been cancelled," I said, staring straight ahead.

"I can't believe mine has!" Annie replied, her gaze following the same direction.

"I was so looking forward to getting away. Being waited on hand and foot." I pictured hunky smooth-voiced barmen and poolside servers in colourful shirts, all happy to attend to my every cocktail need.

"Me too. To have someone else cooking Christmas dinner for once. Or more to the point, to have Emma cooking it."

Keeping our eyes forward, we both sighed, before picking up our wine glasses and simultaneously taking a long, hard swig.

"All to get his money back." I frowned in confusion. "Who lets their girlfriend catch them in bed with another woman and then sticks the boot in for a second time?"

"An argument over a restaurant menu. Who leaves their partner because their lasagne didn't come with a cheese sauce?"

"In a way I blame myself. I should have kept an eye on that booking."

"I definitely blame myself. I've raised a monster."

We both took another drink.

"I don't know what I'm going to do," I said. Having spent nine months insisting I wasn't going to Mum and Dad's for Christmas, I could just see Mum's smug expression at any U-turn on the issue. "My mother's going to be in her element."

"Whereas I know exactly what I have in store," Annie said. "Running around after that daughter of mine, instead of her looking after me. The girl's never done anything for herself." She took a deep breath and slowly exhaled. "I should have known it was too good to be true."

"I hear you," I said.

We clinked our glasses together and downed the last of our wine.

Now in the cold light of day, my thoughts fast forwarded to later in the evening and I cringed, envisaging the stick I was in for when I next saw Annie. Not that I had long to wait, I realised. We were due at work together in less than twenty-four hours.

I didn't have the voice of an angel when sober, never mind when drunk, and as I pictured myself, microphone in hand, belting out George Michael's *Last Christmas* on the karaoke, all the while meaning every single word, I had to ask myself what I'd been thinking. By then, I'd obviously forgotten my woes, stolen someone's Santa hat, and embraced the Christmas spirit, because I was not giving up that mic for anyone.

My stomach lurched, as I recalled myself *Rocking around the Christmas Tree* and screeching through Mariah Carey's *All I Want...* "Someone please kill me now," I said, shamed by the memory.

It was after that sing-along that events got a bit hazy. I'd consumed more alcohol than intended come that point, let alone than was good for me. Then again, as I dreaded to think how the rest of the night had panned out, I supposed a spate of amnesia was for the best.

I should have known better than to drink so much, but a part of me refused to feel bad. After learning that my holiday of a lifetime had gone down the toilet, I deserved a bit of fun. Admittedly, it would have been nice to remember what that fun entailed; especially when for all I knew it could have involved a Charlie Hunnam look-alike. I scoffed, thinking about the Christmas jumper-clad specimens of manhood who had been on offer. "You'd be bloody lucky."

My cranium throbbed again and switching off from the previous night altogether I carried my coffee into the lounge. From the rear window I looked out into the distance, taking in the snow-capped mountain standing proud against a pale grey sky, wondering how long it would be before the village got its first flurry. While I couldn't deny the Yorkshire Dales' natural beauty at any time of the year, I'd always loved its wintery scenes the most. And who knew? Maybe that flurry would turn into a snowstorm and I'd have an excuse to lock myself away until the New Year.

My gaze turned to the numerous walkers, all striding along the well-worn path that cut through the fields leading towards the higher ground. I couldn't help but think them a bit mad considering how cold it must be up there. Although it was the same every weekend; whatever the weather and no matter the season, men, women, and children donned their hiking boots and backpacks and flocked to the village with the sole purpose of reaching that craggy summit. I would have shaken my head if it didn't hurt so much. I'd never understood why anyone would choose to walk all that way to the top, only to turn around and walk straight back down. Then again, I reasoned, they'd no doubt question why I'd pour copious amounts of wine down my neck only to end up fit for nothing the next day – something I had to question too.

Feeling a tad nauseous, I dragged myself away from the window and needing to sit down, I eased my bum onto the sofa, careful to avoid causing myself any more pain. Relishing the quiet, I could have sat there all day, but the silence was broken when my mobile began to bleep. Its flashing light signalled a text had come through. I wanted to ignore it but knew I couldn't, not with Vee almost ready to give birth.

Leaning forward, painfully aware of my every move, I placed my cup down on the coffee table and picked up the phone to see who it was from. Relieved to see Annie's name on the screen rather than my sister's or brother-in-law's, I thanked goodness Vee hadn't gone into early labour. I had enough to think about with regards to my own physical discomfort, let alone anyone else's. My eyes narrowed and squinting as I read, I prepared myself for the teasing Annie was, no doubt, about to give.

Thank you so much for stepping in. You're an absolute life saver. I owe you one.

With no clue as to what Annie was talking about, I stared at her words, trying and failing to figure them out. "You owe me one for what?" I asked. Again, I thought about the previous evening. However, the wine must have been really flowing by the time any need for assistance was mentioned as my mind drew a complete blank. *What had I agreed to do?*

Mystified, I dreaded to think. I had form for acceding to things when drunk. Like the time I promised to steal the local bobby's police car and drive it through the village, blues flashing and twos blaring. And the occasion I said I'd go scuba diving in

Aruba with some German backpacker after he'd finished touring the length and breadth of Britain. Much to my embarrassment, it was a list that went on. Not that I ever made good on such alcohol-fuelled engagements. While everything seemed a good idea after one too many beverages, *sober me* wasn't that stupid.

I consoled myself in the knowledge that whatever I had said yes to couldn't be that bad. Annie wasn't just kind and thoughtful; from her easy-to-maintain haircut to the practical shoes on her feet, everything about the woman shouted sensible. She probably wanted me to have a word with her daughter, Emma, in the hope that I could persuade the girl to forget all about her sauce-less pasta disaster and return home to her boyfriend in time for Christmas.

I took a deep breath, supposing there was only one way to find out, but as my thumb hovered ready to press the call button, the doorbell rang. I cocked my head in response, an action I quickly regretted as it caused my cranium to throb all over again. However, feeling inquisitive as to who my unexpected visitor could be, I disregarded the pain and stuffing my mobile into my dressing gown pocket, I hauled myself back onto my feet and went to investigate.

6

Opening the door, my eyes lit up thanks to the gorgeous chap staring back at me. He was taking off a pair of sunglasses – of all things – in December. The man was obviously a bit of a poser. I put him at about forty years old. He wore a big smile and his wavy blond hair was brushed back off his face. He had a rucksack slung over one shoulder, a guitar over the other and a battered suitcase sat at his feet. Dressed in a fitted jacket, a shirt, and jeans, he cut a smart yet casual figure and forgetting about both my headache and non-event yuletide for a moment, I found myself asking if Christmas had come early.

It was just my luck that a tall handsome stranger would appear at my door when I looked like the angel of death. Suddenly self-conscious, I pulled my dressing gown tight across my chest. I put a hand up and discreetly tried to tame my bedhead hair, with no choice but to accept the fact that the previous night's mascara was, no doubt, smudged down my cheeks. I fixed him with my best smile, hoping his sparkling blue eyes couldn't see that well, hence the sunglasses. "Can I help you?" I asked, curious as to what he was doing there.

He looked confused for a moment, before pulling himself together. "Holly?" he said.

My smile froze at hearing my name. While he seemed to know me, I didn't have a clue who he was. I racked my brains in the hope of figuring out where our paths might have crossed, but try as I might, I still couldn't place him. *Oh, Lordy*, I thought, my tummy doing a little summersault. Maybe I'd met my Charlie Hunnam look-alike the previous night after all. I tried to rein in my excitement, an inner voice reminding me that even if I had met the man of my dreams, I'd never give out something as personal as my address at first contact. "And you are?" I asked, opting to neither confirm nor deny my identity.

"A sense of humour. I like that."

Well-spoken *and* good-looking, I noted, even if I wasn't trying to be funny.

The man's grin grew wider, his smile befitting of any Hollywood star as he dropped his rucksack and guitar at his feet. "You're an absolute saviour," he said, before, much to my surprise, suddenly stepping forward and throwing his arms around me.

Under normal circumstances I'd have quite enjoyed finding myself wrapped in the arms of an attractive gentleman. Particularly when the chap concerned not only looked good but, breathing in his fresh clean scent, smelt good too. However, on that occasion rather than succumb to the embrace, my body stiffened, and I stood there motionless, keeping my arms firmly by my side. Waiting for him to let go of me, I struggled to get my throbbing head around what was happening. As if grappling with the man's identity wasn't enough, he'd given me the added challenge of figuring out what or who I'd saved him from.

My visitor, at last, released his hold and, rather than give him the chance to sweep me up for a second time, I took a quick step back, seizing the opportunity to create some space between us.

"Don't mind if I do," said the man, who, much to my dismay, seemed to misinterpret my action as an invitation to enter.

I stood there opened-mouthed, as before I knew it, he'd picked up his rucksack and guitar and crossed the threshold. "Excuse me," I said, calling after him, but too busy getting his bearings, my words seemed to fall on deaf ears.

"In here?" he asked. Indicating the lounge to his right, he didn't wait for an answer, he simply walked right in.

"But... but..." I said, stuttering. Questioning if the man had a hearing as well as a sight problem, I wondered what he thought he was doing. I closed the front door and raced after him, my brain struggling to compute the fact that a stranger had just let himself into my house.

"Very cosy," he said. Scanning the room, his eyes landed on my crowded bookshelves. "You like to read then?" He dropped his things for a second time and plonked himself down on my sofa, before putting his feet up onto the coffee table. "Very nice."

I struggled to find the right words for what was happening. "What? Who? Why?" I said, followed by a string of unrelated syllables.

"I can just see myself sitting here in front of a roaring fire, Christmas carols playing in the background," he said.

My heart rate increased. The way the man was talking, anyone would think he was moving in.

"Shame there's no decorations about the place though." He turned his head to look at me. "Don't you like Christmas trees?"

As he made himself at home, I didn't only question his actions, I prayed I wasn't about to become a hostage in my own house. Just in case, I told myself the last thing I should do was antagonise the man and wondering how I was going to get him out of there, I decided to play it cool. "It's not that I don't like them," I replied, forced to cough to get rid of the squeak in my voice. "I was meant to be going–" I stopped short, silently scolding myself. Captive or not, I didn't have to give anyone an explanation.

"I get it," he said. "You prefer the real thing. Same here. I can help you choose one if you like?"

I remembered how I'd read somewhere that in order to survive such situations, a victim needed to make their captor see them as a human being. "Like my Mum always says," I said, trying to sound chirpy as I got in the fact that I was someone's daughter. "You can't beat the smell of pine needles at this time of year."

"Well tree or no tree, I can't tell you how grateful I am."

"Grateful?" I said. I watched him get up from the sofa and make his way to the window to look out onto the garden, the furthest point from the door, I noted, in case I had to make a run for it.

"Getting accommodation around here is a nightmare. Especially at this time of year."

So, the man did think he was moving in. *Oh, Lordy.* I closed my eyes, telling myself I must have been dreaming or, thanks to alcoholic poisoning, hallucinating. I flashed them open again. "Accommodation?" I asked.

I breathed a sigh of relief, and almost laughing at my stupidity, relaxed. It was clear I'd been reading too many crime novels. The man before me wasn't a threat, he'd simply mistaken my house for the bed and breakfast down the road. My internal alarm suddenly rang again. Mistake or not, that didn't explain how he knew my name.

"So when Annie said–"

"Annie?" I replied, interrupting him. Confused, I found myself wondering what she had to do with anything. My hand went straight to my dressing gown pocket where my phone sat as I remembered her text message, before recalling our telephone conversation when she said something about having a man problem.

"Don't worry." He turned to face me again. "I'm a good house guest."

House guest? Almost spluttering, I didn't think so.

"I won't trash the place."

As his words sank in, half of me wanted to laugh, the other half to cry and in my silent hysteria, I told myself this couldn't be happening. There *had* to be a mix-up somewhere. I pictured Annie's text telling me she owed me one, but I refused to believe the situation I found myself in had anything to do with my friend. I couldn't have agreed to host a man I'd never met before. I wouldn't. I didn't even know his name.

"It's a shame I won't be here for long though. I mean I'm sure Annie's place is fab–"

"Excuse me?" I wondered if I should query how well he and Annie knew each other.

"But I bet it's not as cosy as this. At least, not with a feisty young woman back in the house." He turned to the window again. "And that view." The man clicked his tongue, clearly impressed. "It's to die for."

I tried to raise a smile, when in truth I wanted to ask him to leave. If he'd never as much as visited her home, Annie obviously didn't know him much at all.

"Anyway, I'm sure you got the story."

While aware that Annie's daughter had landed back home having left her boyfriend, when it came to the rest, I didn't have a clue. And try as I did to remember, thanks to the previous night's alcohol intake everything remained foggy. I cursed myself for drinking so much that I'd lost my memory. Even more so for not living an alcohol-free life. I thought of Annie and felt torn. One part of me was infuriated at being put in this position; the other part was aware there'd be a reason she'd asked for my help.

"Right," the chap said. He rubbed his hands together as if preparing to get organised. "I suppose I should go and get my suitcase before anyone runs off with it." He smiled. "Then you can show me to my room."

I suppressed a squeal.

Heading for the door, he paused and turned to look at me before exiting, his soft eyes and appreciative expression catching me off guard. His stare felt overwhelming, its intensity causing butterflies to play havoc in my tummy.

"Annie said you're a decent sort," he said, at last exiting the room.

I opened my mouth to call after him before changing my mind, instead, pulling my phone out of my pocket and hastily searching for Annie's number. "There has to be a way out of this," I insisted, as I clicked call and waited for her to answer. "Come on, come on." The ring tone continued, yet no one picked up, leaving me no choice but to end the call altogether and repeat the process. "Annie, please."

I suddenly heard voices coming in from the street and closing my eyes for a second, realised my unexpected guest had met one of the locals. I tried to ignore the chatter, but with nothing but radio silence from Annie, I growled, and ended the call for a second time. Despite still being in my dressing gown, I headed to the front door, knowing before I got there which neighbour my unexpected guest would be talking to. When it came to keeping abreast with the comings and goings on the street, the woman didn't seem able to help herself. I was convinced she spent hours at her front window, waiting for an unusual event or new face to turn up.

Stood there in her faux-fur collared coat, perfect make-up, and thick blonde hair that had been straightened to within an inch of its life, Roberta couldn't take her eyes off the man. "If there's anything I can do to make your stay more comfortable," she said. "Maybe show you around the place...?"

He smiled through pursed lips, obviously too polite to dismiss her offer altogether.

"It's not often we get–"

I coughed, interrupting her mid-sentence.

"Oh," Roberta said. "*You're* here."

Going off her tone, my arrival evidently came as something of a disappointing surprise. Not that I could understand why when she was stood right outside my house.

She looked me up and down. "You're looking well."

We both knew I'd looked better.

"Good night, was it?"

I smiled. "Something like that."

"Aren't you the lucky one," she said. "Fin was just telling me he's staying with you for a bit." She fluttered her eyelashes his way.

"Was he now?" I replied, wishing the woman would stop throwing herself at the man and leave. Although I supposed on a positive note, at least I'd been given a name for my unwanted guest.

7

SIX DAYS UNTIL CHRISTMAS

I opened my eyes with a start, forced to concentrate as I listened out. My ears pricked and my pulse raced. There it was again, a noise coming from the landing. "What the...?"

Too scared to go and investigate, I focused as I hunched up onto my elbows, before clocking the chair I'd wedged under my bedroom door handle. The previous day's events came flooding back and remembering my unwanted house guest, Fin, I groaned as I flopped back down onto my pillows. I couldn't believe what *drunken me* had got *sober me* into. With less than a week until Christmas I had enough problems thanks to my cancelled holiday without having to deal with a stranger's housing needs.

My holiday. I'd been so looking forward to doing something not only different but daring for once, and in my small world, life couldn't get any more adventurous than jetting off into the sun solo. I knew, compared to some, my plans weren't exactly out there. But to me, the Caribbean was a planet away from my humdrum existence. To ponder my future in such a far-off place, felt intrepid yet necessary and while Christmas with the family was great, it was nowhere near as exciting. A picture of Jeremy popped into my head. *You bastard!*

I appreciated that life since Jeremy's departure could have been worse. Whereas as some people turned to ice cream and chocolate for solace or, indeed, hit the bottle, I'd *always* had a sweet tooth and enjoyed a glass of red; him leaving had made no difference on that score. In the aftermath of our relationship I didn't need to turn to any substance to help me recover. Anger had been my best friend and while I had to admit that initially I refused to give up my aeroplane seat and hotel bed out of revenge, I'd moved on and learnt a valuable lesson along the way. Rather than assign someone else the responsibility, I was liable for my own happiness. And in a funny sort of way, rather than remind me that my relationship with Jeremy was over, my holiday had represented the beginnings of a new relationship – with myself.

The sound of the shower running filtered into my room, shortly followed by Fin's dulcet tones as he began to sing. I scowled. The man might've been able to hold a tune, but it was far too early for *We Three Kings.* In fact, as I checked the time on the clock next to my bed and realised my alarm wasn't due to go off for another half an hour, it was far too early for anything.

I wondered what he was doing up at that time of the morning. Unlike me, I presumed he didn't have work to go to and as he carolled, I grabbed the sides of my pillow and pulled them forward, pressing the padding against my ears to drown out the noise. However, it was no match for Fin's voice, I could still hear every word, and I pulled the pillow from behind my head altogether and threw it towards the door. Not for the first time since Fin landed, I decided that no matter what predicament Annie was in, or why she'd asked me to put him up, the man had to go.

Finally, the singing stopped, as did the running water from the shower. For what good that was, by then I was wide awake. I listened intently for a while and thanks to the silence, supposed I should get up and ready for work. After all, it wasn't as if I was going to get back to sleep.

Throwing the duvet back, I climbed out of bed and put on my dressing gown. Then I tiptoed to the door and carefully removed the chair from under the door handle, pausing for a second to make sure all was still quiet. The last thing I wanted was to bump into Fin on the landing. Concluding all was clear, I let myself out and approached the bathroom. "Jesus!" I said, jumping out of my skin as the door flew open in front of me.

Fin stopped in his tracks, and going off the look on his face, he was as surprised to see me as I was him. "Good morning," he said, quickly recovering.

"Good morning," I replied, my voice a little higher than I would have liked.

Standing there, he wore nothing but a big smile, a twinkle in his eye, and the tiniest of towels. His damp hair was pushed back from his face and droplets of water lay scattered across his bare chest. If I'd thought the man was good-looking when dressed, he was even more gorgeous with no clothes on. Keeping my eyeline up, it was all I could do to keep my gaze from wandering downwards.

"I want to apologise for yesterday," Fin said. "I didn't mean to be rude and disappear like that, but once I saw that bed, I couldn't help but test it out. You know what it's like after a long journey? A five-minute snooze turned into an all-nighter."

I swallowed hard. Unused to strange men in my house at the best of times, let alone *persona non grata* of the half-naked variety, words failed me. My heart rate sped up and I suddenly felt hot.

"Okay then," Fin said, clearly not sure how to deal with my muteness. He waited another second or two before speaking again. "Can I?" he asked, indicating his desire to get past.

"Sorry. Yes," I said, finally finding my voice. We both stepped to his left, then his right, and then his left once more, leaving Fin somewhat amused and me feeling a tad extra flustered. "Sorry," I said again and with no choice but to step away from the door altogether, I rolled my eyes in an exaggerated fashion, a feeble attempt at making light of the situation. "After you."

Watching him head to his room, I took in the man's broad square shoulders and strong frame, and blowing my overgrown fringe away from my eyes, I, at last, allowed my gaze to drop. Admiring his bum, pert and perfectly defined under his towel, my uterus felt like it was about to burst into flames and as I ogled his taut muscular thighs, I let out a little whimper. Fin's whole mien was a sight to behold.

Fin turned and looked my way. "Thank you," he said, winking at me, before disappearing into his room.

His gesture shook me out of my trance and feeling embarrassed, I couldn't believe his cheek as I hastened into the bathroom. Annoyed at myself as much as I was with him, I locked the door behind me, flicked on the shower and set it to cold. The man had to go.

Having showered and dressed, I readied myself for a busy day at work. I loved my job as a bookseller, but there was no denying it was hard on the feet. The run-up to Christmas was especially frantic, another reason why my holiday would have been much appreciated. I could have done with R and R. I sighed, plonking myself down on the bed. With time running out and still not sure what I was going to do over the festive period, I needed to come up with a plan of action. Then again, as I put on my shoes, I supposed I had more pressing matters to deal with first. Like getting rid of Fin.

The smell of something cooking wafted upstairs and into my room. Narrowing my eyes, I jerked my head and looked to the door, unable to believe Fin was making himself breakfast. Making breakfast meant he'd rummaged in my cupboards. Talk about taking liberties.

Bristling, I grabbed a hair bobble, piled my hair on top of my head and secured it in place, all the while asking who Fin thought he was. "First, he wanders up and down the landing like some Greek god," I said. "And then he commandeers the kitchen." I fumed at the man's audacity for clearly making himself at home. I paused in my thinking, realising I may well have described the perfect man. "Perfect, my arse," I said, dismissing the idea. In my experience, when it came to men there was no such thing.

My irritation continued as I headed downstairs to the kitchen. But I stopped in the doorway, staring at the table, surprised by what I saw. Fin wasn't just cooking for himself. The table was laid for two, completed with a little vase containing a sprig of heather from one of my garden pots.

"Just in time," he said.

I felt a bit guilty as he smiled my way, frying pan in one hand, spatula in the other.

"I hope you're hungry."

I stood there, gobsmacked at the lengths he'd gone to. Apart from on the odd occasion when I ate out, no one other than family had ever cooked for me before. Not even Jeremy and he'd practically moved himself in.

"Breakfast is served," Fin said.

Watching him plate up the most delicious looking start to the day, I thought about the limited food stuffs in my fridge. Eggs, cheese, and a half bag of spinach. Fin was clearly some kind of culinary wizard, able to make something out of nothing.

"Come on," he said. Indicating it was time to eat, he placed the empty pan on the stove. "Before it gets too cold."

I took a seat at the table and feeling impressed by his efforts, picked up my knife and fork.

"It's frittata," Fin said. "An Italian dish. Or as I like to call it, posh omelette."

Stuffing some into my mouth, I didn't care what it was called, it smelt divine and was blooming mouth-watering. Slightly firm on the outside with a seductive ooze in the middle, as soon as the flavours and textures hit my taste buds, I groaned in delight. "Beats a bowl of cereal," I said.

Fin laughed. "Glad to hear it."

As I tucked in, I sensed Fin's eyes on me and feeling self-conscious I stopped chewing to return his gaze. I put a hand up to my chin to make sure I didn't have a string of cheese or rogue piece of spinach hanging off it. "What?" I asked.

"Nothing."

He seemed to have the same look in his eye that Mum had when Vee and I were growing up. Be it a mug of home-made soup or a dish of ice cream, Mum liked nothing more than to see her children enjoy their food. It was as if our delight at the meals put in front of us somehow reciprocated the love that she'd put into preparing them.

"It's good to see a woman enjoying her food for a change, that's all. Instead of pushing it around her plate pretending to eat."

"No chance of that here, I'm afraid," I replied with gusto. "When it comes to food, I don't have that kind of willpower."

Fin laughed. "Glad to hear it." He, at last, began to eat too.

Silence descended as we both concentrated on our food and after a while, an awkwardness began to settle. I knew why, of course. Sharing a breakfast table had an intimacy to it, yet Fin and I were no more than strangers. Wondering if he felt uneasy too, I snuck a peek at Fin, only to find him looking at me in return. He held my gaze longer than necessary and finding myself drawn in, I forced my eyes to look away. "Where did you learn to cook like this?" I asked, shaking off the moment. "Because this is *not* like any omelette I've ever tasted before."

"I'm surprised Annie didn't explain. She told me all about you. I loved the bit about you wanting to be a novelist, by the way."

My blushes were twofold. Firstly, I hadn't got around to even trying to follow that dream of mine. And secondly, I knew Annie would have told me everything about Fin, I just couldn't remember. And after thirty-six hours I doubted I ever would.

"It's my job. I'm a chef."

"Well going off this you're obviously very good at it," I replied. "I'm impressed."

Fin smiled to himself, seemingly glad of the compliment.

Keeping my attention on my food, one inner voice told me it was a shame Fin would be gone by the end of the day. I could have got used to having a professional cook on the premises. Another voice told me it was probably for the best that he wasn't staying. If he could rustle up something so simple yet lip-smacking for breakfast, goodness knew what pleasures he conjured for an evening meal. The man might've been a culinary magician, but my bones were big enough.

Looking over at Fin again, I sensed the whisperings of a third voice trying to interject, but I refused to let it speak.

8

Thanks to Fin, I might have had a full belly, but that didn't stop me feeling the cold when I set out for work. Jack Frost had left a blanket of white in his wake and as I stepped out onto the street, with my duffle coat buttoned up tight and a thick scarf around my neck, my breath steamed forth in recognition.

Scraper in hand, my fingers went numb as I chipped away at the ice covering my car windscreen, clearing it for the drive. By the time I climbed in I was shivering, and the temperature inside the vehicle was no better than the temperature outside. Placing my bag on the passenger seat, I put the key in the ignition and turned on the engine, whacking the heater up to full as I pulled out.

Blowing into first one hand to try to warm it up, and then the other, I took in the landscape as I drove. I loved living out in the sticks but while I could never deny the place's wintery beauty, I had to admit there was a harshness to country life at that time of year. Sheep, with their thick weather-sodden fleeces, huddled together, grouped against drystone walls, and trees stood frozen and leaning thanks to freezing temperatures and the prevailing wind. What appeared to be the perfect Christmas card scene from the comfort of my little cottage seemed less enamouring when slipping and sliding behind the wheel of a car.

Dropping into town, I still hadn't warmed up and I lamented that I wouldn't be escaping to the sun any time soon. However, pushing my gloom to one side, I knew I had the issue of Fin to sort out before I could concentrate on coming up with another plan for Christmas. The sooner I talked to Annie the better.

I pictured Fin and I sat at the breakfast table. Me looking at him, him looking at me... I could still feel the power of his gaze. It was a strange experience. In that moment, his presence had felt intense as if there had been a kind of connection between us. I knew I hadn't imagined it, yet at the same time I couldn't explain it.

I told myself it was probably the result of seeing the man half naked. It had been a while since I'd been that close to a hot-blooded male. I'd obviously breathed in too much testosterone. Besides, there were bound to be weird encounters between him and me. While theoretically Fin had been invited to stay, thanks to my memory loss in practice he'd turned up out of the blue. We were two strangers thrown together under one roof. I'd had no time to mentally prepare.

I sighed. "Or I could just fancy the man?" I said, yet another complication I could do without, especially when for all I knew he could have a wife and three kids.

By the time I pulled onto the car park, a huge square in the centre of town that served as a marketplace every Tuesday, I was determined to tell Annie that Fin couldn't stay. That was if I got the chance, I realised. Seeing the number of people already milling about, it was clear I'd be lucky if I got a five-minute break, never mind the opportunity to sort out my home life. Gathering myself for a busy day ahead, I switched off the engine, grabbed my bag and disembarked, being careful not to slip as I made my way over to the shop entrance.

Once inside, I glanced around in search of my friend among the customers and fellow employees dotted about the place, but Annie was nowhere to be seen. Heading straight for the staffroom to get rid of my stuff, I was surprised to find she wasn't there either and I began to feel anxious. *Was I stuck with Fin?*

I shed my coat and scarf and hung them both up, wondering if I should be worried about Annie too. Putting my bag in my locker, I frowned. It wasn't like her to be running late; she was the most punctual individual I knew. And unlike some, Annie was never sick, lame or lazy. I looked at the wall clock and hoping everything was all right, decided to sneak in a quick call to check on her while I had the chance.

"There you are, Holly," Ruth, the shop manager said, popping her head into the room just as I was reopening my locker ready to phone Annie. "Will you be long? It's getting busy out here."

My shoulders slumped. "Just putting my stuff away," I replied. Company rules dictated no mobile phones during work hours and with less than a minute before my shift started the last thing I wanted to do was to admit breaching policy. "All done," I said, securing my things away for the second time. Telling myself that Annie was fine, she was simply running a bit behind and that I could talk to her later, I followed Ruth back out onto the shop floor.

"Let the fun commence," she said, leaving me to deal with my first customer.

Everyone and their dog seemed to cross the threshold that morning, eagerly scanning the shelves, Christmas present lists at the ready. There was a buzz in the air as customers came and went. Tills rang to the sound of Christmas songs playing in the background and shelves were restocked as quickly as they were emptied. While not every member of staff appreciated days like that, I loved them. Even more so when dealing with customers who, in searching for a gift for a valued friend or relative, didn't know where to start. Sharing recommendations and talking all things literary with book buyers was the best part of the job and whatever the genre, I could have waxed lyrical all day long when it came to giving advice. As far as I was concerned being a bookseller didn't just pay the household bills, spreading a love of books was a vocation. Not quite the same as having my own titles on the shelves but spending my days amongst other literary greats came a close second.

"Looks like we're on the same lunch break," a familiar voice said in my ear.

In the middle of tidying up my section, I turned to find Annie, tapping on her wrist, as if reminding me of the time. "When did you get here?" I asked, relieved to see her. Having been non-stop busy since the start of my shift, I hadn't even noticed her come in, yet there she was, wrapped up in her coat ready to leave again. The morning had clearly flown by.

She held my coat and scarf out to me. "I thought we could go across the road for a bite. Enjoy a change of scenery for a while. My treat."

Despite her smile, I could see Annie didn't feel as upbeat as she hoped to portray. Her tone sounded a little too bright, as if belying the fact that what she really wanted to do was to let out all her woes. I smiled back with a less than ingenuous smile of my own, hoping the conversation I needed to have with her about getting rid of Fin wasn't going to be one problem too many for Annie to handle. But I wouldn't know that until we sat down and talked.

I pictured breaking the news in our stark soulless staffroom, cup of coffee in one hand, a floppy sandwich in the other. That versus the conviviality of the café, with its cheery customers, welcoming staff, not to mention its mouth-watering menu. "Over the road it is," I said.

9

Leaving the shop behind, Annie and I scuttled passed the giant Christmas tree that dominated the town square and shops festooned in twinkly lights and snowflake-stencilled windows. The temperature was as cold as it had been when I'd left for work and our breath fogged in front of our faces. Like youngsters, we linked arms, holding on to each other as we walked to prevent either of us slipping on the icy ground. The way things had turned out of late it would have been just our luck if one of us skidded and fell, breaking a leg in time for Christmas.

"I love this place," I said, bringing Annie to a halt outside the bakery-come-café and, taking in all the goodies on display, I sighed at the deliciousness before me. If I didn't work in the bookshop, it was safe to say working there would have been my next choice of employment. My eyes went from the snowball madeleines made with butter cake rolled in jam and coconut, to the whisky crumble mince pies, adorned with star shaped lids and dusted in icing sugar. It was all I could do to keep my tongue off the glass. I swooned over the cranberry and ginger tiffin, covered in sweet white chocolate, and the spiced biscuits, shaped like stockings, reindeer, and angels, all of them intricately decorated. It was a visual feast and I couldn't decide if the place was heaven or hell for a food lover like me.

"You wouldn't get any of this lot in the Caribbean," Annie replied.

I scoffed. "And that's supposed to make me feel better, is it?"

Annie laughed. "Every cloud..." She tugged at my arm and dragged me towards the entrance. "You go and sit down," she said, as we stepped inside.

"But I don't know what I want yet."

"I'll surprise you."

"I won't argue with that," I said, happy to do as I was told. With so much choice, it would have only taken me ages to decide what to have. Plus my feet ached from a busy morning and with an afternoon of work still to go, they needed all the respite they could get. I took off my coat and scarf and headed for a window table, although when I got there, I couldn't see the street beyond as the glass was steamed up. Taking a seat, I drew a smiley face in the condensation, before turning my attention to fellow diners.

Christmas carols played in the background and people chatted over festive spiced coffees, and clove-infused teas. They tucked into savoury puff pastries, stollen, and chocolate-dipped honeycomb. My belly rumbled at the assortment of snacks and treats being eaten and I looked over at the counter, pleased to see Annie at the front of the queue.

Annie turned and approached with a tray of delights – two mugs of hot chocolate, each topped with a mountain of cream and marshmallows, and two huge sticky muffins.

I felt my eyes light up.

"Tangerine and marzipan flavour," she said, handing one of the cakes to me. "I thought the sugar rush would keep up our energy stocks for the rest of the day."

"Isn't it carbs that are meant to do that?" I said. Although I didn't care either way. Eager to accept the offering, I'd have taken sweet over savoury any day of the week.

Annie placed my drink in front of me and set the empty tray to one side.

"I'm ready for this," I said, picking up my accompanying spoon and scooping up a mouthful of cream from my drink.

"Me too," Annie replied.

I sat there pensive, trying to decide how best to approach the subject of Fin. Annie looked tired which made me reluctant to dive straight in and tell her she had to find Fin alternative living arrangements. Wanting to tread carefully, I thought it best to take a more casual approach and work up to it. "So how come you were late in today?" I asked.

"Oh, don't." Annie came over all animated, throwing herself back in her seat and waving her hands around as if glad of the opportunity to get everything off her chest. "You won't believe the morning I've had. All thanks to that offspring of mine."

I smiled at the nameless reference to her daughter. It reminded me of Mum. To that day, whenever Vee or I did anything wrong, as Mum outlined our misdemeanours to Dad we weren't described as their children, we became his and his alone.

"First, she uses up all the shampoo, so when I get in the shower I can't even wash my hair. Then I get in the car and she's used up most of the petrol." Annie peeled away the paper that encased her muffin. "Not that I realised. Which is why the bloody thing came to a standstill halfway into work. So guess who had to walk the rest of the way?"

My heart went out to Annie as I imagined her, red-nosed and shivering, trudging through the cold, cursing her daughter with every step. I felt guilty in the knowledge that I was about to make her day more difficult, even if I was trying to choose the right moment. "I bet that sorted out the cobwebs," I said.

"That's one way of putting it." She picked up her knife and began cutting her cake in half and then half again. "Honestly, the sooner she moves back in with that boyfriend of hers, the better."

Offering me just the inroad I needed, I opened my mouth to ask when that might be, but before I got the chance, Annie started speaking again.

"It obviously wasn't enough that I'd spent the whole weekend picking up after her."

I watched on as Annie's muffin cutting became more aggressive, the more she talked.

"Two outfits she wore yesterday. Two! And did she hang the first one back up or put it in the washing basket after changing? Oh, no. She dropped it in the middle of the landing so muggins here could sort out where it went."

I was tempted to tell Annie about how I was serenaded with a Christmas carol at the crack of dawn that morning. I wanted to see Annie her pile of clothes and raise her the half-naked man I'd found on my landing. But thanks to her disposition and the knife in her hand, I thought better of it.

Annie paused to look at me. Her tangerine and marzipan muffin looked like it had been hung, drawn, and quartered. "You don't realise how much you appreciate your own space until it's invaded, do you?"

I wanted to seize the opportunity and tell her I knew exactly how she felt. I wanted to say my friend was lucky, because she hadn't had to wedge a chair under her bedroom door handle for fear of being murdered in her sleep. I wanted to highlight the fact that when it came to Emma, at least there was no chance of Annie's kitchen being commandeered, and that while Annie's daughter might infuriate her, Emma wasn't someone whom Annie knew nothing about.

"Thank goodness she'll be gone tomorrow."

"Tomorrow?" I said, trying not to come across as quite so eager.

"The day after that at the latest."

"So, two days from now?" Any relief I'd felt began to fade.

"She hasn't left him for good. She can't have. Not over lasagne," Annie said.

"No. She definitely can't have done that." I was trying to reassure myself as much as I was my friend. But it seemed Annie didn't have a clue about when her daughter would be heading back to her own house and I felt panic at having a stranger in mine.

Annie's mobile phone bleeped from inside her bag. "This will be her now," she said, as she began rooting for it. "I know it will."

I watched her face tighten as she read the message.

"What normal person wants ice cream in the middle of winter?" Annie lifted her gaze to look at me. "Can you believe she wants me to pick some up on my way home from work."

Knowing Emma, yes, I could.

"Like that's going to happen." Annie slung her phone back in her bag, the woman's despair on show for all to see. "I could swear she does these things on purpose just to get at me." She took a deep breath as if trying to rid herself of her stress. "I'm sorry. I don't mean to whinge. I'll shut up now."

I tried to raise a smile. "Not on my account, I hope," I said, any opportunity to discuss Fin's presence in my house fast disappearing.

"No, I mean it. Enough about me and my misery. Let's talk about what's going on with you. Have you managed to sort out another holiday?"

"Actually, I wanted to talk about–" I tried to get back to the problem at hand but Annie interjected.

"And what about Fin? How is he?"

"He's–"

"Good, I hope. I really should've spoken to him by now. Arranged to meet up."

Going from one topic to another without waiting for an answer, Annie's mind seemed to be all over the place and the last thing I wanted to do was send her into even more of a spin. Deciding to put the issue of Fin moving out on hold, I clung on to Annie's suggestion that he'd be gone in a couple of days. "He's fine as far as I know," I said. I pictured him the last time I saw him, flitting around my kitchen. "He certainly didn't say anything to the contrary this morning."

"Over breakfast?"

"Yes."

"What do you normally have for breakfast."

"A bowl of cereal."

Annie raised an eyebrow. "And this morning?"

Wondering why the questions, I opened my mouth to reply.

"No. Don't tell me." She put a hand up to stop me. "He cooked for you, didn't he? This is so not fair. When I think about the morning I've had. I knew I should've sent Emma your way, not him." She paused to look at me direct. "Do you know how lucky you are?" She sighed. "I bet he's as gorgeous as ever too, isn't he?"

I envisaged Fin, wearing nothing but a towel, every muscle and ripple on show. My nether regions tingled. "He's not bad, I suppose."

Annie looked at me, incredulous. "Not bad! I think you're doing the man a great disservice."

I laughed. "All right, he's very handsome."

I stirred the last of the cream into my hot chocolate, thinking

I should at least know a little bit about the man seeing as he was staying with me for a couple of days. "So tell me again," I asked, trying to sound nonchalant. "How do you know Fin?"

"He's Elliot's cousin. From the posh side of the family."

I considered the way Fin spoke, how his words sounded clear and rounded. His enunciation couldn't have contrasted more with the flat Dales dialect I was used to. "That explains the accent."

Annie laughed. "Lovely, isn't it? Although his branch is nothing like the one I married into. Anyway, I haven't seen him for years, not in person. Not since the funeral actually, and even then I didn't expect him to come."

I supposed that explained why Fin had never visited her house.

Annie appeared thoughtful for a moment. "Good of him, considering. Although he and Elliot were quite close once of a day, so I suppose I shouldn't really have been surprised."

I didn't know Annie back then, so I never had the honour of meeting her husband in person. By all accounts he was a well-loved man and people often talked about him. I could appreciate why Fin would have wanted to pay his respects.

"Fin's an only child," Annie continued. "He used to come up and stay with Elliot's family during school holidays, which apparently, he loved. I got the impression his parents weren't as hands-on. Children should be seen and not heard, kind of thing."

"That seems sad."

"Elliot reckoned it didn't do Fin any harm. It's what makes him able to focus." Annie furrowed her brow. "I thought I'd told you all this."

I shifted in my seat. "It doesn't hurt to have information confirmed."

Annie's frown turned into a grin. "You don't remember any

of what I said, do you?" She giggled. "I know we drank a lot that night, but I told you to keep quiet, not forget. This is hilarious. Boy, are you in for some fun." She had a glint in her eye.

"Keep quiet about what?" I asked.

Annie's smile remained. "Nothing," she said, putting a piece of decimated tangerine and marzipan muffin into her mouth.

10

It was dark by the time I got home. Pulling onto the drive, I turned off the car engine and lights and sitting there for a moment resigned myself to the fact that my house guest wasn't going anywhere for the next couple of nights.

I contemplated the evening ahead. My feet ached and I was talked out thanks to the myriad customers I'd dealt with at the bookshop and the last thing I wanted to do was to spend the evening entertaining Fin. I took off my seat belt, stuffing the last-minute gift Annie had given me into my bag. A thank you for having Fin stay, she'd said as she handed it over at the end of our shift, in a kind, yet unnecessary, gesture. I climbed wearily out of the vehicle, hoping Fin wouldn't mind takeaway for dinner. Not that he had much choice. I had meant to call at the supermarket on the way home, but in the end I couldn't face more crowds.

As I let myself into the house, the delicious smell of something cooking hit my nostrils and breathing in the appetising aroma, I relaxed a little. After a busy day at work, it was a welcome surprise to know I had one less thing to worry about and if Fin was trying to earn his keep, he was doing a very good job. Goodness knew what meal he'd managed to throw together though as the last time I looked the cupboards were bare. While I'd realised at breakfast that the man was a culinary magician, dinner had clearly taken his alchemy to another level. I took a deep breath and, readying myself to play hostess with the most-ess, fixed a smile on my face, just as Fin appeared at the top of the stairs.

"Your bath's ready," he said, making his way down.

"What? You've run one for me?"

He chuckled as if such an act was nothing.

"Fin, I could kiss you right now."

"After a busy day at the Christmas coal face I thought you might be ready for a good soak."

"Strike that," I said. "I could snog you." I wondered why I couldn't see his wings. As far as I was concerned, the man was an angel.

He reached the bottom step and took my bag and coat, all the while meeting my gaze. "Dinner first, dessert later."

Speechless, I simply stood there as Fin turned and headed down the hall. Almost swooning, I had to question why I'd spent the last twenty-four hours determined to get rid of him. I told myself I'd died and gone to heaven and sighed at my evening's good fortune. He might have been joking about afters, but an attractive man, catering to my every other need... what other explanation was there?

"Don't be too long," he called back. "Dinner will be ready soon."

Fin disappeared into the kitchen and I trudged upstairs. Already undressing by the time I entered the bathroom, I paused, surprised by the serenity that greeted me. It was like walking into my own little spa. The only lighting came from the vanilla-scented candles dotted around, while the tub brimmed with glistening bubbles. A big fluffy towel hung warming on the heated rail, and I had to smile at the glass of wine sat on the corner of the bath. Fin had thought of everything.

I pondered for a moment, wondering if the man was for real. Good looks, confident personality, thoughtful, not forgetting his sense of humour. There had to be something wrong with Fin somewhere, no one was that perfect. I supposed if he did have any flaws, they were bound to show themselves at some point. After all, if Fin was play-acting, the longer he stayed, the harder it would be to maintain any pretence.

I sighed as I looked around the bathroom again and taking in Fin's efforts, wondered if I was just being cynical. After all, not all men were selfish pricks, Dad and Mitch were proof of that. I pictured my father giving Mum a foot rub despite her not having the most attractive of feet. And I'd often seen my brother-in-law massage Vee's back when the strain of carrying their baby took its toll. Fin was obviously of the same ilk.

I felt a twinge of jealousy as I imagined Fin preparing a bath for someone he loved instead of me, the woman he was merely showing gratitude to. It saddened me to think I hadn't yet bagged my very own Fin, that my experience hadn't been positive when it came to members of the opposite sex. In fact, the only men I could've truly relied on were the ones I was related to. I shook my head. It was no wonder I was jaded.

Stripping the rest of my clothes off, I couldn't wait to climb into the bath. I took a deep breath and exhaled in pure bliss as I lowered myself into the water. Leaning back, I felt my muscles relax. I appreciated the efforts my house guest had gone to – whether the man was genuine or not. As I lay there, a part of me wished he could stay forever, while another warned me not to get used to such pampering.

Fin is here for a couple days, it said, *and a couple of days only.*

11

―――――

"I hope you're hungry," Fin said. He smiled as I entered the kitchen.

"Famished," I replied, feeling the most relaxed I'd been since his arrival. Wearing my pyjamas and with a towel wrapped around my head, I took a seat at the table.

"Glad to hear it. There's enough to feed a banquet." He turned to look at me again. "Don't get too excited though, it's nothing special. Your little village store isn't exactly bursting with choice on the ingredients front."

"Let's just say the locals are a traditional bunch."

"The meat and two veg brigade, eh?"

I sniggered. "Something like that."

As Fin got back to work, it began to feel a bit strange just sitting there. Aside from twiddling my thumbs, I didn't know what to do with myself while he flitted around sorting dinner. Not used to being waited on, especially in my own kitchen, it was as if I was a guest in my own home. "Anything I can do to help?" I asked, straightening myself up, hopeful.

"No, everything's in hand."

I slumped down in my seat again and glancing around,

looked for a distraction. Noticing my bag hanging over the back of my chair, I remembered Annie's gift and thought I may as well open it. Pulling it out, I knew my present was a book before I'd started unwrapping. However, tearing at the paper, I was surprised to see the back of a cookbook. It was a strange present considering I'd never shown the slightest interest in developing my epicurean ability. *It must be Annie's idea of a joke*, I thought, remembering the breakfast conversation we'd had at lunch. Flipping it over to look at the at the front, I froze, before putting a hand up to my mouth to stop a squeal from escaping. I looked from the book to Fin, glad he was too busy making dinner to clock my horror. *It can't be.*

I hadn't been that shocked by a piece of reading material since I picked up a newspaper a few years prior, only to find Mum and Dad plastered all over the front page. There they were, staring back at me, looking like a pair of glum Santa's little helpers after being threatened by the local council.

Having decided the time had come to hold their own Christmas light switch-on, it seemed Mum and Dad had opted for the same date that the local council had organised theirs; a double booking that probably wouldn't have been a problem had the Noelle family home not attracted more visitors. To be fair to Mum and Dad, their offering did outdo the tree and three or four lines of brightly lit streamers the authority had put up in town and under those circumstances, it shouldn't have come as any great surprise to find certain numbers lacking. As a result, it seemed the local council felt they had no choice but to slap an injunction on Mum and Dad, thus preventing them from hosting any such events in the future. Hence, the reason for the newspaper article. Of course, Mum and Dad relished in the public outpouring of support. However, for me personally, such civic backing was more of a curse than a blessing, on account of it cementing my parents' reputation as number one on the eccentricity scale.

Returning my attention from Fin to the book, it was clear the image I stared at had been photoshopped. The laughter lines evident on Fin's actual face had been smoothed out and the golden glow to his skin lightened. There was no hint at his confident, cheeky manner; in the picture, stood there with his arms folded and wearing chef whites, Fin appeared the consummate professional.

My heart raced as I flipped the cookbook back over and scanned through the blurb, reading about how Fin had cooked for royalty, both regal and Hollywood alike. I saw words like *world-class* and *renowned* followed by a whole list of appearances on American TV shows. *Oh, Lordy.* There was even a mention of a recent stint as a judge on a top UK cookery programme. I swallowed. *Why did it have to be that programme?* The show might have been new, but from the very first episode it had taken the nation's cooking aspirations by storm; everyone, bar me, seemed to watch it. I recalled all the conversations I hadn't been able to join in with. The themes of the week, the food combinations, the gorgeously handsome judge. *Oh, bugger.* He was only stood in my kitchen.

"What have you got there?" Fin asked, glancing over from the stove.

I stuffed the book back into my bag before he could see it. "A gift from Annie," I replied, trying to keep calm. "A book she thought I'd be interested in."

"That's kind of her," he replied with a smile.

"Isn't it?" I said, imagining her sat at home laughing to herself, at the same time knowing I'd be freaking out.

I told myself to calm down and carry on as normal. Although as I watched him get back to his cooking, I had to wonder why he'd kept quiet on the career front. I began to feel affronted, all the while insisting it didn't matter to me what Fin did for a living, so what if he happened to be the most famous judge on UK television? Did he think I'd play fangirl just because he was on the telly? Did he think I'd throw myself at him? Like that was ever going to happen. I silently scoffed. It just went to show how little the man knew me.

I struggled to maintain my indignance, unable to reconcile the man I'd just described with the man I was observing. The Fin in front of me had shown no signs of being egotistical or superior; he'd been nothing but generous. The man had run me a bath for goodness' sake.

I glanced at my bag, wishing I hadn't stowed his book away like that. Not facing him with it meant I had to keep his secret too; something I wasn't sure I could manage.

"The shop owner seemed a nice woman," Fin said.

My pulsed quickened. Shop owner, Karen, the woman who watched every cookery programme going. Karen, one of the nosiest people in the village. I began to panic. "So you spoke to her then," I asked.

"Not really. She just seemed very polite."

Oh, Lordy. Not usually one for good manners, the woman had clearly recognised him.

I knew Fin's presence would be all around the village. Between Karen and Roberta... *Oh, no*, I thought, suddenly recalling Roberta's weird response to Fin. *That's why she was staring. She knew who he was.* Looking back the clues kept coming. *And the sunglasses he wore. They were obviously a disguise.* A bad move on his part, I realised. Shades in the middle of a depressing Yorkshire Dales winter didn't exactly render the wearer inconspicuous. I began to freak even more, picturing desperate housewives and cookery wannabees queuing down the street.

12

_____

"**V**oilà!" Fin said, laying a plate in front of me. "Shepherd's pie."

I tried to show some appreciation as I looked from my dinner to him, but the shock of finding out Fin was the nation's current TV darling was still affecting me. I took in the creamy mashed potato, browned to perfection; the bed of minced beef, covered in a rich mouth-watering onion gravy; and the heap of puréed carrots that brought the dish a bit of colour. "Perfect," I said, mustering a smile even if my usual healthy appetite had all but gone. "Although I _really_ wish you hadn't," I added, thinking about Fin's trip to the shop. "We could have ordered something in."

"I wanted to. My way of saying thank you. It can't be easy having your space invaded like this."

If I'd thought having an unexpected house guest was bad before, it suddenly seemed a whole lot worse. "Don't be silly," I said. "It's fine."

Picking up my fork, I thought about the breakfast Fin had made, the bath he'd just treated me to, and the dinner I was trying to eat. I knew I'd said I wanted some excitement in my life, but having a famous chef running around after me wasn't quite what I'd meant. "You do know they'll have you down as my live-in lover? And by now, the news will be all around the village."

"I'm okay with that if you are?" Fin replied, accompanying his words with a great big smile.

I felt my cheeks redden. Having half hoped and half expected him to run for the hills at such a prospect, I was surprised to find he quite liked the idea.

"Dig in," he said, indicating I should eat.

Doing as requested, I realised I had no other choice than to accept the situation and I told myself if he didn't have a problem with gossip, then I shouldn't either. He was the TV star and had more of a reputation to lose than I did. If anything, I garnered a bit of kudos out of the situation. Besides, real life could be boring, I asserted. So what if people thought I was partaking in a *histoire d'amour* with a man celebrated for his cooking?

My heart sank. Who was I kidding?

Imagining the tittle-tattle, my enthusiasm began to wane. Recalling past events in the village, I didn't think I'd ever forget the spotlight old Mrs Harper found herself under when her husband died. The locals weren't always kind with their words, despite everyone knowing the woman had wanted that new patio of hers for ages.

"It's all right for you," I said. "I still have to live here after you've gone."

I fell quiet, wondering why Fin hadn't revealed his identity. Did he miss having anonymity and was enjoying the chance to be himself for a while? Did he have trust issues? The latter being a bit rich considering I'd blindly given him a bed.

Pushing my food around, I snuck a look at him, aware that the man's behaviour was no different now than it had been that morning and I scolded myself for thinking his fame changed things. Since landing, Fin had been nothing but thoughtful, valuing the fact that I hadn't claimed there was no room at the inn and that he'd have to go and find himself a Christmas stable. And it wasn't as if I'd been totally honest with him either. I hadn't shown him the cookbook and faced him with his stardom; I'd kept it to myself, just like he had. Feeling like a hypocrite, I took a deep breath. "I have a confession to make," I said.

"Really?"

"I haven't been totally upfront."

Fin put his fork down, giving me his full attention. Gone was the man's confidence, Fin looked nervous, scared even, as if he knew I was about to out him as the world-class chef he evidently was.

His expression made me feel selfish. Questioning who opening my mouth benefited, I realised it wasn't my place to out him of anything. "I don't remember inviting you to stay," I said, instead.

Fin's mien relaxed; his relief palpable.

"I did, of course. Invite you, I mean. To help Annie out. I just didn't know that when you turned up. I've got amnesia, you see, after drinking too much. Which is what can happen when someone drowns their sorrows. But you're still welcome to stay. Until Annie's spare room becomes vacant again." I knew I was rambling, one of the things that happened when I fibbed. "If you want to, that is."

"So, you let a random stranger into your house without knowing anything about them?" he asked.

I nodded.

"You're one special lady," Fin said.

A part of me hoped he'd follow my lead and own up to his secret. But it was clear he had no intentions of confiding in me about anything. I was disappointed, wondering why he didn't trust me, when I'd just put myself at risk of him thinking I had a drink problem. On top of trusting him enough to let him into my home, I hastened to add. I recalled the chair I'd wedged under my door. Well, I'd sort of trusted him.

"I meant to ring Annie today actually," he said, moving the conversation on. "To find out what's happening with Emma. I got sidetracked with emails and organising work stuff though, so never got around to it."

With Fin staying schtum, I knew I had no option but to go with the flow and two days from then, Fin would be a thing of the past anyway. "There isn't much to tell apparently," I replied. "Although Annie assures me you'll be able to move into hers in a couple of days."

"Assures you, you say. Should I be offended?"

I let out a chuckle, realising how that must have sounded, and considering his fame, I wondered how many people dared speak to him that way. "I didn't mean it like that."

Fin smiled in return, looking me straight in the eye and unable to translate his expression, I felt myself blush. "You need to do that more often," he said.

"What?" I asked.

"Laugh."

Deciding I didn't care who the man was one way or the other, I stuck my tongue out at him in response. If Fin wanted a slice of ordinary life with ordinary people, then he could have it. I dug my fork into my dinner and scooped up a mound of shepherd's pie. "This is delicious," I said, my appetite back.

"So why the need to drown your sorrows? If you don't mind me asking?" he said.

I thought about the previous few months and the awful time I'd had thanks to Jeremy. And as much as there were aspects of Fin's life that he didn't want to share with me, I realised that there were parts of mine that I preferred to keep to myself too. "I was meant to be going away for Christmas."

"Annie told me. To the Caribbean, no less."

"It was cancelled on me. Last minute."

"Ouch!"

"I know."

"So what will you do?"

Having not had the chance to think about it, I still wasn't sure. "Suck it up, I guess. It's not as if I'll get in anywhere else at this late stage."

"No family to go to?"

I nodded. "Yes, but I was hoping to give them a miss." It would have been easy to say sod it, I would spend the day at Mum and Dad's like always. Mum especially would have loved that. But while, as solutions went, doing a U-turn was great in the short term, it was nowhere near the right thing in the long. Trying to get Mum used to the idea of me not being around that year had been tough enough and should another opportunity to do something different one Christmas further down the line arise, the last thing I wanted was to go through the whole rigmarole again. Which is what I knew would happen if I didn't see some alternative plan through.

"If it helps ease the blow, Christmas on your own isn't all it's cracked up to be. Believe me, I know. There have been times when I'd have given anything to be able to do the whole family thing."

I recalled Annie describing his parents as aloof, at the same time telling me Fin was an only child. I couldn't help but think he must have had a lonely childhood and picturing him as a little boy, I felt sad for the man. "Yes, well," I said. "You haven't met my lot, have you?"

He smiled. "For what it's worth, if you don't know what to do, my advice is don't do anything."

Continuing to eat, I mulled over his words, before jolting up in my seat. Suddenly alert, a spark of an idea formed in my head. "I think you've hit on something there," I said.

"What do you mean?"

I began to feel excited. "Well only you and Annie know my holiday isn't going ahead, right? If the three of us keep it that way, I can just stay here. I can hibernate for the duration."

Fin laughed. "That's not what I meant. I was talking about in the interim. Until you figure things out."

"Obviously. But don't you see? Locking myself away is perfect. I don't have to lose face when it comes to Mum. She's always hated the idea of me going away for Christmas, by the way. And while I might not be surrounded by sun, sea, and sand, I'll get the peace and quiet I've been looking forward to. The headspace to think."

I saw myself lounging about the house like some lady of leisure, reading book after book, with no one but myself to please. I saw myself penning ideas for a novel while wearing my maxi navy-blue boat neck dress. I could eat chocolate for breakfast, lunch and dinner if I wanted to. For the first time since learning my holiday had been cancelled, I began to look forward to Christmas again. I grinned. "It's gonna be great."

There was a knock at the door. *Ding Dong Merrily on High* suddenly rang out as carol singers gave it their all.

I smiled. "It's a sign," I said, glancing through to the hall. "That I'm doing the right thing."

Fin shook his head, his accompanying laugh making it clear he thought I was mad.

13

FIVE DAYS UNTIL CHRISTMAS

Thank goodness for twenty-four hour supermarkets, I thought as I stood at the bottom of the stairs putting on my coat. I didn't usually go shopping at close to midnight, especially after a hard day's work and another shift the following morning, but having decided to lock myself away for Christmas I thought it safer. The last thing I wanted was to be spotted doing a festive food spree and word getting back to Mum and Dad. As far as they and the rest of the world were concerned, I was still going on holiday.

I grabbed my bag and shopping list, stuffing the latter into my pocket. I'd scoured the internet for the odd Caribbean meal to make during my staycation, intent on photographing the dishes to prove to Mum and Dad I was eating well during my alleged trip. Fin still thought I was barmy for even considering spending Christmas on my own. Plus, I got the impression he thought I'd neither cope nor pull it off. I giggled. "Oh, ye of little faith."

The front door opened and Fin appeared from outside. He wore a hoodie under a thick jacket and a pair of woolly gloves. I looked from him to the living room, confused. I hadn't seen him leave. "Where have you been?" I asked.

"Getting the car ready? Are we all set?"

I frowned at the word *we*. "You can't come with me," I said.

"Why not?"

My mind raced as I tried to come up with an excuse. I couldn't tell him he had to stay home because I stood no chance of remaining inconspicuous with the star of the biggest UK TV cookery show pushing my trolley. Every wannabee chef or fangirl housewife in the store would recognise him and both our secrets would be out. I had to say no for his sake as much as mine. "Because I'll be quicker if I go on my own," I said. Cringing at the feebleness of that statement, it was the best I could come up with.

"Have you even cooked Caribbean food before?" Fin asked.

"No, but I have recipes and I've written down everything I need." I pulled out my shopping list to show him. "See."

"I'm impressed," he said. "Although I'd have happily helped with this. All you had to do was ask." He scanned the piece of paper. "Do you even know how to check if a pineapple is fresh or not?"

Whether I did or didn't, he still wasn't coming with me. "It doesn't really matter as long as it looks the part. I'm only making one or two dishes to throw Mum and Dad off the scent. I'll be enjoying my usual diet most of the time."

"Well what about a Brussels sprout. Do you...?"

"Yes!"

"Come on, Holly. You might not want my help, but I can at least keep you company on the drive. It's the middle of the night; what if someone tries to carjack you?"

I laughed. As excuses went, that one was as bad as mine. "I don't know where you've been living for the past few years." I did, of course. According to his book blurb, he'd been in the US.

"But this is the Yorkshire Dales and I assure you, we've yet to have our first car theft at gunpoint."

He looked at me like I was a miserable parent out to spoil her child's fun. "Please?" he said, through puppy-dog eyes.

"All right," I said, my resolve crumbling. "You can come with me. But we're straight in and straight out."

Fin appeared satisfied but I was less than happy. It wasn't just his presence that bothered me; it was all the cakes and bakes I planned on treating myself to, all the less-than healthy options that Fin was bound to raise an eyebrow at. "And no judging," I said. "It is Christmas."

He laughed in response as we headed outside.

True to his word, the car engine was running and the windscreen de-iced. I shivered as I locked up behind us and headed for the vehicle. But I was forced to pause before climbing in because Fin was staring up at the heavens.

"Stunning," he said, taking in the thick blanket of stars.

I recalled the blurb on the back of his book again which detailed his time in Hollywood. Having also read somewhere that Los Angeles was prone to smog, I thought it no wonder the man was mesmerised. I followed his gaze and recognising Alnitak, Alnilam, and Mintaka, the three stars that make up Orion's belt, I acknowledged its wonder. Although having never experienced anything *other* than a bright, glittering night sky, I had to admit I didn't pay it much attention as a rule. Constellations were just something I'd learnt in school. "Time to go," I said.

In spite of the ungodly hour, Fin was clearly pleased to be getting out and about as he climbed into the passenger seat and I appreciated why. He must have been going a bit stir-crazy stuck in the house. The only place I'd known him to go since landing was the village shop and while probably not the same as visiting a Farmer's Market or organic food fair, for a foodie like him a trip to the supermarket had to have felt like the next best thing.

As I pulled away to begin our journey, I was dying to ask Fin about his job. I might never have watched it, but being a part of the biggest UK cookery show must have been an exciting experience for him. I bit my lip, knowing I couldn't. Not least because the longer I'd left telling him about the true nature of Annie's thank-you gift, the harder it had become to mention. Plus, I knew if Fin had wanted me to know about the more dazzling side of his career, he would have told me. In fact, thinking about it, Fin hadn't said much about anything.

I wondered why he wasn't in a relationship as Fin hadn't talked about one of those either. From what I'd seen of him, it was hard to believe the man was still single. "So how come there's no Mrs Fin?" Having thought that aloud, I immediately wished I hadn't and feeling mortified, prayed he hadn't heard me. Staring straight ahead, my eyes drilled through the windscreen and my face flamed red. I couldn't believe I'd let such words out of my mouth and I thanked God it was dark so Fin couldn't witness my embarrassment. *Someone kill me now*, I silently said.

"Why do you ask?" Fin replied. "Is it a position you're interested in?"

Finding Fin's question even more embarrassing, I blushed deeper. I turned to look at him, aghast, but he didn't return my gaze, his simply sat there, face forward, his expression deadpan. "You wish!" I said.

His face broke into a smile and telling myself I should have known the man was teasing, I relaxed and gave him a playful nudge.

He twisted round in his seat slightly to position himself more in my direction. "If you really want to know, I suppose I've been too busy building a career to even think about starting a relationship."

"That's a bit boring, isn't it?" I said.

"What can I say? Working in a kitchen involves long hours, which doesn't leave much time for socialising. Although even if I had been lucky enough to meet the right someone, taking things further wouldn't have been fair. I've seen too many couples crack under the strain of not seeing each other that much."

"That's sad," I said.

"Maybe. But it's the way it is." He paused before speaking again. "So, what's your story? Why is there no Mr Holly?"

I laughed. "My reasoning is less complicated. I'm single because when it comes to the men around here, I'm surrounded by idiots."

"Harsh!" Fin replied.

"But true."

"There must have been someone at some stage," Fin said. "A gorgeous woman like you."

"Now you're teasing again," I replied. "But, yes, there was. A couple of someones actually, although not at the same time of course."

"Of course."

"I'm just not the kind of woman who likes to share her man."

"Duly noted."

Enjoying the banter between us, I tried not to smile. "Good to know."

"Cheaters?" Fin asked.

I nodded. "Oh, yes." As I concentrated on the road, that was all I wanted to say on the matter, something Fin seemed to appreciate and fell as silent as I did. However, I could feel his eyes still on me. "What?" I asked, keeping my gaze forward.

"I wasn't teasing just then," he said. "You *are* gorgeous. And everything *has* been duly noted."

He turned in his seat to face forward again, while I burned red once more.

14

Usually when I stepped out of the car, I'd be hot footing it indoors, all the while shivering thanks to the cold. However, on that occasion, as I stepped out into the wintery open air, I saw no need to rush. Making our way to the supermarket entrance, I felt warm and fuzzy. During the drive, I'd played Fin's words over and over in my head and even though I tried to insist he didn't really think I was gorgeous, there was something in the way he spoke that gave me butterflies.

As we neared the doors, Fin pulled his hoodie hood up, an action that made me smile. "What?" he said, clocking my amusement. "It's cold."

I knew it had more to do with him trying to hide his identity and I had to admit it did quite a good job on that front. As for rendering him inconspicuous, that was debatable. Rather than rocking the Hollywood heart-throb image, he appeared more shoplifter chic. Not the best look considering where we were heading in to.

I grabbed one of the giant trolleys before going inside – a trolley I fully intended on filling. Like Dad had said, I only had myself to think about; and my stomach planned on taking full advantage.

Fin took charge of the trolley, at the same time smiling the way I had only seconds prior.

"What?" I asked. Not only was I doing a Christmas shop and picking up all the goodies that entailed, I had to get enough supplies to see me through the whole of my staycation and no way was I risking running out of anything.

Making our way down the first aisle, I took in the assortment of colour that greeted us. Packed full of fruit and vegetables, it was a feast for the eyes as much as it was the mouth. To the right, boxes of dark red cherries, crates of huge dimpled oranges, and a mountain of deep purple figs were just some of the wares on offer. While to the left, carrots sat next to parsnips, red cabbages, green Brussels sprouts, and goodness knew how many varieties of potato, all of which I could imagine roasted or glazed alongside everything else on my Christmas lunch plate.

Fin dove in, picking up and putting down fruit and veg after fruit and veg, all the while prodding and squeezing.

"What are you doing?" I asked. "Other people have to buy those."

He dismissed my concerns. "When it comes to food, you look with your hands as well as your eyes."

I pulled out my list so we could share shopping duties and between us we began searching the displays for limes, plantains, sweet potatoes, and fresh herbs. Just some of the ingredients I needed for my first foray into Caribbean cooking, I couldn't wait to challenge my culinary talents. "I hope you're going to give me some tips before you leave," I said. "These dishes not only have to taste good, they have to look authentic for the camera too."

"I thought you'd never ask," Fin said.

I watched him pick up a huge golden pineapple. "Go on then," I said to him. "Show me how it's done."

He smiled. "Ripe pineapples typically have a sweet smell near the base." He put it to his nose and sniffed. "See?" He held it my way, inviting me to do the same. "If it doesn't have any odour, it's probably not completely ripe."

"I'll take your word for it," I said, unable to smell anything at all.

As we moved on, meandering up and down the aisles, Christmas shopping in the early hours was a relaxed affair. Unlike during the daytime throng, there was no jostling for position to get to the shelves or negotiating the dodgy-wheeled trolleys that seemed to freeze mid-aisle for no apparent reason. There were no stressed-out conversations as people struggled to find the last box of sage and onion stuffing, or screaming children wanting to taste every sweet treat in sight.

We sang along to the Christmas classics that played in the background without being judged and staff chatted amiably amongst each other as they restocked supplies. The supermarket was like chill-out heaven and as the very few fellow customers smiled at me and me at them, Fin turned his face away pretending to focus on the shelves as he walked. We strolled from one aisle to the next, perusing and choosing from the festive fare at will.

As the trolley got fuller, my stomach felt increasingly neglected and scanning the rows of goodies for sustenance I reached for a tin of chocolates. I tore off the packaging, opened the lid and took one out.

"And you had the cheek to ask me what I thought I was doing," Fin said.

I knew from experience I could eat as I went; as long as I handed over for scanning what would, no doubt, be a container of wrappers by the time I got to the till. Balancing the chocolates in the trolley child seat for convenience, I eyed the Christmas puddings and tossed one in with the rest of my shopping. "That'll do nicely," I said.

I took a moment to glance at my list again, to make sure Fin had picked up as many essentials as I had treats. "I'll read them out," I said, "you tell me if we've got them."

"Go for it," Fin replied.

"Basmati rice?"

"Check."

"Coconut milk?"

"Check."

"Honey?"

"Check."

"Nutmeg, cinnamon, and allspice?"

"Check."

As we went through the list, I looked forward to putting together dishes like sticky jerk salmon, rice and peas, and sweet potato and black bean curry and scanning down the ingredients, the trolley seemed to hold most of what was needed for an authentic Caribbean diet.

"It looks like we're about there," I said. As Fin grabbed the trolley handlebar ready to continue, I just had to hope any snapshots of my efforts were enough to fool Mum and Dad.

I smiled as we began to move on, having thoroughly enjoyed shopping with Fin. I fantasised about us being a couple, getting ready for our first Christmas together until a lone shopper halfway up the aisle to my right caught my attention. I narrowed my eyes, feeling sure I knew her, but couldn't for the life of me place where from. I told myself I had nothing to worry about. She was way too young and far too fashionable to know Mum and Dad. She had the shiniest dark hair, a gorgeous figure and, wearing the skinniest of skinny jeans, legs to die for...

"Oh, no," I said. My heart missed a beat, a huge part of me

wishing she had been an acquaintance of my parents. "Not here. Not tonight."

15

Recognising the woman as Jeremy's bint, I slowed my step and not wanting to face her, prayed she didn't turn around and spot me in return. I didn't think I could cope with any more of her gloating. Every time our paths crossed, she'd smirk, as if she were stood on a podium and my ex was the gold medal. It didn't seem to matter that she'd won him by default on account of me throwing him out.

I was tempted to make a noise simply to get my own back. I knew if she looked over and saw who I happened to be out shopping with, her smile would be well and truly wiped. I also knew that wouldn't have been fair to Fin though and feeling stuck, I felt the colour drain from my face. I seized Fin's arm, bringing him and the trolley to a standstill.

"What is it?" Fin asked, clearly noticing my pallor.

I considered beating a hasty retreat, but not only was the trolley too full for a 180-degree rotation, Fin would want to know why the sudden change in direction. He'd start to ask questions that I didn't want to answer. I'd have to explain all about Jeremy and how I caught him in the act and who with. That experience alone was embarrassing enough without having to give Fin the juicy details. "We've forgotten shampoo," I said, hoping I sounded more casual than I felt. "Would you mind popping back for some?" At least if I was on my own I'd stand a chance of getting out of the situation with at least some dignity still intact.

"Sure," he said, although I could see he was suspicious. "Any particular brand?"

"No," I replied, wishing he would just go before the woman saw us. "I'm not fussy. I'll meet you in the next aisle, shall I?"

Clearly knowing something was afoot, Fin looked up and down the aisle we were on. "Okay," he said, obviously failing to see anything untoward from his point of view. "If that's what you want."

Leaving our shopping with me, I watched him re-trace his steps back down the way we'd just come, waiting until he'd disappeared around the corner before returning my attention to Jeremy's new woman. I took in the mountain of food piled high in the trolley, compared to the healthy products in her little basket, consoling myself in the fact that at least she was on her own and that I didn't have Jeremy to contend with too. I thanked goodness that she was too engrossed in her own shopping requirements to notice me and mine. I took a deep breath ready to push on and while she appeared to compare product consumer labels, I grabbed the trolley handles having decided to try to sneak passed.

I tried to look relaxed, and taking a leaf out of Fin's book, pretended to glance at the shelves to my left as I went. Picking up pace, I managed to overtake the woman and the end of the aisle reached touching distance. With only a ninety degree turn to go, I knew I'd soon be out of sight and I prepared to breathe a sigh of relief.

However, with a tonne of goods in my trolley, I struggled to slow the damn thing down, let alone manoeuvre it around a bend. Thanks to the weight of my shopping, the trolley seemed to take on a life of its own, veering first left and then right and then left again. I grappled to get it under control, forced to keep one hand on the handle, while using the other to prevent the trolley's mountain of food spilling everywhere. Unable to see where I was going, I tried and failed to make the turn, and crashed head on into a shelving unit. Coming to a sudden halt, cereal boxes rained down on me, just as Jeremy rounded the corner.

"Holly," he said, looking aghast at the mess I'd caused.

I flinched as a final packet of cornflakes ricocheted off my head.

Staring back at him, I'd often envisaged what it would be like coming face-to-face with Jeremy again, but never in my mind's eye did I ever conjure up the situation I found myself in. In my imaginations I was off to some posh event, all dressed up, wearing perfect hair and make-up; in fact, I'd never looked so glamourous. Naturally, upon seeing my beauty Jeremy realised what he was missing and begged my forgiveness. And with no intentions of giving it, my response was detached yet polite. I had, after all, moved on...

What my make-believe scenario didn't include was me embarrassing myself thanks to breakfast cereal. I wanted to flee, but my feet refused to move, and my pride wouldn't let me. "A bit of help wouldn't go amiss," I said instead, indicating the carnage around me.

My request clearly caught him off guard and he looked over to his bint as if torn about what he should do.

Following his gaze, I could see the woman was still immersed in her reading and, shaking my head at her selfish obliviousness, I returned my attention to my ex. "Please!" I said, a word that must have sounded like an order as I'd never seen the man move so quick.

"Yes, sorry," he said, getting straight to clearing up my mess.

Watching him, I felt powerful. As if tidying up after me was the least he could do after the way he had treated me. I thought it a shame he couldn't have been quite so helpful when we were together. Back then, he was slow to pick up after himself, let alone anyone else. He began to huff and puff as he worked, and his face began to redden. *What had I ever seen in him?* I hadn't realised how unfit the man was before, or noticed the bald patch on the top of his head. A picture of Fin's swept back locks and half-naked physique popped into my mind. Taking in Jeremy's increasing sweatiness, I couldn't help but compare.

"Jeremy," his new woman called out. "What are you doing?" She began walking towards us.

My stomach sank. Although I should have known she'd turn around at some point.

Jeremy flushed red. "I'm just helping–"

By then the woman was upon us. "Oh," she said, looking straight at me. "It's you."

Unlike my ex, she'd never had the decency to blush in my presence. Then again, I supposed, why would she? Knowing I'd seen more of her naked body than I'd wanted to, I assumed my seeing her in full attire didn't really compare in the embarrassment stakes. "Well this is awkward," I said. At least it was for me.

She stared at the food in my shopping trolley, before turning her attention to Jeremy, glaring at the man, suspicious. "I thought you said she was off to the Caribbean for Christmas? And that's why we couldn't go?"

Did he now? I thought. *That's interesting.*

"She is?" he replied. He flashed me a look as if willing me to keep my mouth shut.

"Well it certainly doesn't look that way," his new woman said.

As Jeremy, too, took in the mountain of food in my trolley, I wondered how he would excuse my shopping expedition. Especially when he knew as well as I did that he'd cancelled the holiday to get his money back. However, it seemed Jeremy expected *me* to do his dirty work for him, as both he *and* his bint trained their eyes my way expecting an explanation. As I looked from him to her, I couldn't believe their gall. His downright lies and her downright arrogance made it clear they really did deserve each other.

"I can't think why you'd say that, Jeremy," I said, feigning surprise. I turned my attention to his bint. "He told me the reason I couldn't go was because he was taking you."

The bint's eyes widened, her fury evidently building.

I looked to my ex. "Didn't you?"

Jeremy began to splutter, but no matter his denials the woman was having none of it.

Grabbing my trolley's handlebar, not only did I feel satisfaction, I knew it wouldn't be long before Fin was back with the shampoo. "Anyway, I must dash," I said ready to go and meet him.

Jeremy and his new woman clearly didn't hear me. By then they were too busy arguing.

"You bastard!" his new woman said.

"Honestly,' Jeremy replied, "I don't know what she's talking about."

Leaving them to it, I smiled, surprised to find that manoeuvring my shopping suddenly seemed a whole lot easier. "Have a great Christmas," I called back. "Because I know I will."

16

Having arrived at work early, I had the staffroom to myself and although I knew this was just the calm before the Christmas shopping storm I felt energised, ready for a busy book-selling day. There were three reasons for my good mood: it was my last shift before Christmas; I'd managed to get one over Jeremy and his new woman; and, finally, Fin's hearty, yet fun, breakfast. I smiled as I thought about the lengths Fin had gone to that morning, wondering if there was no end to his culinary talents.

Under normal circumstances, I'd have been quite miffed about someone raiding the spoils of my late-night shopping trip. However, Fin didn't just plunder the cupboards for the ingredients to make the fluffiest of pancakes, he did it to make the fluffiest of *Rudolph* pancakes. Using bacon for antlers, cherries for eyes, and a plump juicy strawberry for the reindeer's nose, the dish was a smile on a plate. Although my breakfast did come with a lecture about the freshness of the strawberries and cherries I'd snuck into the trolley, which according to Fin must have been imported, rather than home-grown, because it certainly wasn't the UK's strawberry and cherry season.

I shook my head, still able to hear his sermon. In my view, what did it matter if the fruit was flown in? Then again, I reasoned, despite Fin's tutoring I still didn't know a fresh pineapple from a dud, even when it was stuck under my nose. And neither was I a world-renowned chef.

As I made myself a cup of coffee, my thoughts returned to the day ahead. It was Secret Santa day and having drawn Annie's name out of the hat, I had the perfect gift wrapped and ready to go under her tree. I pulled the gift out of my bag and placed it on the table ready for her, chuckling as I imagined her face when she opened it on Christmas morning. The perfect cookbook payback.

I looked forward to my last shift of the year and though I wasn't celebrating in any traditional sense, I felt full of Christmas cheer. If all went to plan, that evening Annie's house would be a daughter-free zone. And with Emma moving out, that meant Fin could move in and my staycation could begin in earnest.

I pictured Fin's smiling face, telling myself it was funny how quickly I'd got used to having him around. My optimism waned slightly. He might have only been with me for a few days, but I'd still miss him.

The quiet was disrupted by chatter filtering into the room before the door opened and my colleagues sauntered in. They talked about their plans for the upcoming holiday and listening to them, it seemed, like me, they couldn't wait for their time off to come around.

"It's all about the food and drink in my opinion," Richard from non-fiction said. He rubbed his rotund belly. "As much turkey, stuffing, and real ale as my stomach can take."

"Don't forget to leave room for plum pudding," Janice from holiday and travel said. She appeared to come over all dreamy.

"Smothered in hot brandy sauce... I'm getting hungry just thinking about it."

"There's always room for a bit of dessert, Janice," Richard replied, with a laugh.

"Well I'm hoping for something special this year," Samantha from children's said. She giggled as she raised her left hand and wiggled her ring finger.

"Oh, that's wonderful," Janice said.

"About bloody time, you mean," Richard said. "How long have you been seeing him now? I was beginning to think he was gonna leave you sitting on the shelf."

"Richard!" Samantha and Janice said in unison. They simultaneously nodded in my direction; an action that lacked the discretion I was sure they'd gone for.

Although their response came as no surprise. In a place like the Yorkshire Dales, everyone seemed to know everyone's business, Jeremy's affair and the reasons I'd needed a new mattress included. Ever since word got out, I'd been a woman to be pitied and I'd had nothing but tea and sympathy from those two for months.

"Don't worry," I said, making sure to sound like the lonely, dejected spinster they had me down as. "Just because my love life's non-existent, that doesn't mean I can't be happy for someone else."

Richard coughed, clearly embarrassed at the alleged faux pas. "Apologies, Holly," he said.

It was at times like that that I felt sorry for the man. He'd never seemed comfortable at even the slightest of sexual references, however innocent, which unfortunately for him seemed par for the course when working in a group like ours.

"So, what will you have for Christmas lunch?" he asked, evidently keen to move the conversation on to a more acceptable subject – food. "I suppose you'll be on rice and peas or something?"

His accompanying expression looked pained, as if he couldn't think of a meal worse, although I'd long had the notion he was one of those people who took a suitcase of food on holiday because they didn't like anything foreign. "Something like that," I replied. Having never been any good at telling fibs, I flashed everyone a smile and hoping I didn't appear as awkward as I felt, it was my turn to want a change of subject.

"Make sure you bring back lots of photos," Samantha said, still in her own little lovestruck world. "I might very well be looking for a fabulous honeymoon destination come New Year." She giggled again. "And you can't get any more fabulous than the Caribbean, can you?"

"You certainly cannot," I said, acknowledging the increasing pressure being put on the quality of the food snapshots I planned on taking.

"I can't imagine ever going away for Christmas," Janice said, scowling. "At least not somewhere hot. I much prefer the cold this time of year. It's more festive."

"I'm sure the Australians would disagree," I said, wondering why on earth Janice had been put in the holiday and travel section.

"Christmas in sun," she said, shaking her head. "It doesn't bear thinking about."

The staffroom door opened, and we all looked round to see Ruth, the shop manager, breeze into the room. "Sorry, folks, it looks like we're a staff member down today." She headed straight for the coffee machine. "Annie's had to take the day off."

Richard groaned at the news. Out of everyone, he had always been the most work-shy.

"Not to worry," Ruth said, upon hearing the dissent. "Between us we're more than able to pick up the slack."

Richard muttered something under his breath.

"After all," Ruth continued. "Annie's never had a problem stepping in for one of us when called for." She turned, focusing her pointed gaze on Richard. "Has she?"

"Nothing serious, I hope?" Janice asked, her tone going up at the end of her question.

I rolled my eyes. Like most of the local folk, she did like a bit of gossip.

Ruth, who was a stickler for staff confidentiality, looked at Janice like she should have known better. "Not too serious, no," she replied, drinking a mouthful of coffee.

While Janice tutted in disappointment, Samantha focused on her ring finger, and Richard frowned at the extra workload, I smiled at the news of Annie's absence. Ruth might not have said anything, but unlike the others, I had a pretty good idea why Annie needed the time off. If what she'd said over lunch the other day was true, Annie would be ferrying her daughter and her daughter's belongings back to where they belonged: safe and sound in the home Emma shared with Josh.

"Right," Ruth said, as she checked her watch. "Time to get to it."

Unlike my colleagues who remained slow to move, I jumped up from my seat and headed for the door, ready to embrace the morning ahead.

"Come on, come on," Ruth said, clapping her hands at the others. "These books won't sell themselves."

"Holly," Ruth said, calling me back as the others began filing out of the room.

I stopped in my tracks and turned to look at her.

"Before you disappear, can I have a quick word."

"Of course," I replied. I suddenly felt nervous, wondering what I'd done wrong to warrant such special attention. After all,

I must have done something. Ruth only ever wanted one of her little chats when all wasn't well.

My colleagues looked at me, their eyes questioning. But as much in the dark as they, I shrugged my shoulders in response. I watched Janice slow her step, as if no one would notice her loitering.

"Chop-chop, Janice!" Ruth said, her voice stern. She waited until dawdler Janice was out of sight and earshot before speaking again, despairingly shaking her head at the woman before she could, at last, turn to her attention back to me. "It's nothing to be concerned about, I'm simply passing on a message while I can still remember."

"Okay," I replied, unsure as to what the message could be.

"You know what it's like around here when it gets busy, everything goes clean out of your mind. Anyway, Annie asked if you could give her a ring?"

"Really," I said, surprised. I didn't have a clue what could be so important she'd asked Ruth to play intermediary. Especially when Annie could have easily rang my phone and left me a message. "Did she say why?"

Ruth shook her head. "Nope. Just that she needs a favour."

I considered the last time Annie needed my help; on that occasion I ended up with an unexpected house guest.

"I haven't a clue what it entails, I'm afraid. Although I hope I'm not speaking out of turn when I say it probably has something to do with her daughter."

"Probably," I replied. *Poor Annie*, I thought. Emma did tend to expect an awful lot of her mother.

"Anyway, I said you'd ring at around half-ten, when you're on your morning break." Ruth tilted her head and smiled. "Don't look so worried, it'll be something and nothing."

I smiled back, telling myself that Ruth was, doubtless, right. Emma might have only been at her mum's for a few nights, but knowing Annie's daughter, the odds were she simply had too much stuff and Annie needed a bit of help to shift it all.

"So, I can leave that with you?" Ruth asked.

I nodded.

"Good," Ruth said, efficient as ever. "In the meantime, we've got work to do."

17

————

Time usually flew by when the shop was busy. But despite dealing with one customer after another, my morning break seemed to take forever to come around. Since talking to Ruth I'd carried around a nervous anxiety no amount of self-reassurance could shift. The last thing I wanted to hear was that Emma wasn't going home yet. My staycation couldn't go the same way as my holiday – down the pan. Wrapped up in my coat, with a cup of coffee in one hand and my phone at the ready in the other, I could just imagine Mum's face if I had to do a U-turn on Christmas and spend it with the rest of the Noelles, after all.

I headed for the shop exit, having decided to make the call to Annie away from prying eyes and piqued ears. I couldn't risk the likes of Janice overhearing our conversation only to put two and two together to make six. "I won't be long," I called out to Ruth.

Busy dealing with a long line of customers at the till, she looked my way and stuck up her thumb in acknowledgement.

I shivered as I reached the door and stepped out into the open air. The numerous shoppers, weighed down with bags as they trudged about the square, appeared as miserable as I felt.

Some kept their heads low as they went from one store to the next, while others chatted amongst each other. Their red noses, woolly hats, and sheepskin mittens reminded me that I only had lowering temperatures to look forward to that Christmas, instead of the balmy days and nights that should have lain ahead. Turning my attention to my phone, I scrolled down the screen in search of Annie's number, all the while pacing up and down and sipping on my drink, trying to keep warm.

No sooner had I hit the call button and Annie had answered. "Holly?" she said, "Have I got news for you."

A far cry from the doom and gloom she'd expressed over lunch a couple of days prior, the excitement in Annie's voice surprised me. I immediately relaxed and breathed a sigh of relief, pleased to hear all was well and that I'd been fretting over nothing.

"Emma's pregnant," she said, before I got the chance to speak.

I stopped still. "Excuse me?" Whatever I'd expected to hear, it wasn't that.

"I know. Isn't it fantastic?"

"Wow," I said, needing a second to let the news sink in. "Since when?"

"About three months, which explains why she lost the plot over a lasagne," Annie said.

"And where her sudden yearning for ice cream came from," I said.

"Exactly. To be honest I feel a bit guilty over that. I put it down to Emma being her usual self, the possibility of her expecting didn't even cross my mind. Although I don't know why I didn't realise. The food issues I had when I was carrying... They obviously went down the lead." Annie laughed. "Or should that be umbilical cord?"

"Maybe I should feel bad too then? I do have a pregnant sister, not to mention a very well-read brother-in-law."

"Please tell me he's still information sharing."

I recalled the last time I saw Mitch. I'd called round to see Vee who wasn't just cleaning the house when I got there, but deep cleaning it. *Nesting*, Mitch called it, before giving me a long-winded explanation about how mums-to-be tended to tidy and clean their house more as they approached their due date.

"He is," I replied.

"Good. Because I might need someone to hand when things get a bit much with Em." Annie squealed in delight. "I can't believe it, Holly. I'm going to be a grandmother. Talk about the best Christmas present ever."

I smiled, pleased for my friend. "When's the baby due?"

"Not until early summer, which gives me plenty of time to dust off the old knitting needles."

My friend's joy was infectious and imagining her clicking away with two pointy sticks and a big ball of four-ply, I chuckled in response. "I shall look forward to seeing your creations. And what about Emma? How does she feel about it all?"

"She's happy, of course. Although admittedly it's taking a bit of getting used to. She and Josh didn't exactly plan on starting a family so soon."

I couldn't say I was surprised. Emma took a carefree approach when it came to most things in life.

"And daddy-to-be?"

"Strutting around like a peacock." Annie laughed. "The poor lad hasn't a clue what he's got in store. Emma can be a pain at the best of times, but pregnant Em... it's going to be one hell of a ride."

I sympathised. Having met Josh a few times, it was evident he was perfect for Annie's daughter and not just because they made a cute couple. Yes, he was polite and had the boyish good looks to match Emma's beauty, and as the saying went, opposites attract, but when it came to Emma and her dramatic tendencies, Josh's patience wasn't just admirable, it was never-ending. If they gave out medals for tolerance, that young man would be on the podium collecting gold, and I'd have been cheering him on for an award he wholeheartedly deserved. "I'm sure he'll be fine," I said.

"And they'll have me for support," Annie replied.

"They? You mean Emma and Josh have sorted things out?" Amongst all the excitement, I'd momentarily forgot about everyone's living arrangements. "They're a couple again?"

"Yes, thank goodness." Annie sounded as relieved as I felt.

Instantly, I looked up to the heavens and mouthed my heartfelt *thank you* to the universe. "That's wonderful," I said, pleased to know I could start looking forward to Christmas again. A staycation might not have entailed heading off into the sun, but it did save me from losing face in front of Mum.

Aware that it was because of Fin, I felt a chink in my delight. I knew I'd miss the man and not just for his cooking. On top of his culinary expertise, I enjoyed his banter, his smile, and especially his compliments and just thinking about the way he'd looked at me sometimes made me come over all tingly. Then again, sharing my living space with a man as famous as him and not being able to talk about it hadn't been easy and the longer he hung around, I supposed the harder that would get. I told myself he was probably moving on to bigger and better things soon anyway. The last thing I needed was to fall for someone who was just going to up and leave at some point. The important thing was securing my staycation.

"Which brings me to the reason I asked you to call."

"Ruth said you needed a favour and whatever it is, despite your little joke over the cookbook–"

Annie's laughter interrupted me. "I'm sorry. But when I

realised you'd forgotten what I'd told you I just couldn't resist. What did he say when you showed it to him? Did he see the funny side?"

"I didn't show him."

"Why not?" Annie sounded disappointed.

"Because he hasn't got a clue that I know who he is." I began pacing up and down again. "And I don't want to embarrass the man."

"You mean, he hasn't said anything himself?"

"Nope."

"Now that is interesting."

I stopped still again. "What is?"

"The fact that he's kept schtum."

In my view, there were lots of reasons why Fin would have kept the details of his career to himself. Reasons I'd considered over and over again since Annie had given me his cookbook. From wanting to protect his private life, to not feeling the need to brag. Not to mention all the pitfalls in between. The media was littered with kiss and tells and celebrity horror stories about lives going wrong because either they, themselves, or the people around them hadn't kept a level head. Fin's silence could simply be a means of keeping himself sane.

"It means he likes you," Annie said.

"Why would he not?" I asked. "I'm a lovely person."

Annie laughed. "I don't mean he likes you. I mean he *likes* you."

As much as I wanted to believe Annie, I scoffed. "Rubbish. We both know that man could have any woman his heart desires, and I assure you, his heart most certainly doesn't desire me."

"He wants you to get to know Fin the man. Before you find out about Fin the famous TV chef."

I chuckled. Whereas I read a lot of crime fiction, Annie

preferred a wholly different genre. "I think someone's been reading too many romance novels," I said.

"I'm telling you. It's how these things work."

Shaking my head, I'd never heard anything so ridiculous. "Back to the favour," I said. "Whatever it is, it's a yes from me. See it as a gift, to celebrate becoming a grandparent."

"Really?"

Considering we were best friends, her surprise surprised me.

"You don't know how happy I am to hear you say that. Honestly, it's like a weight's been lifted. I was dreading having to tell Fin he'd have to find a hotel. You know what it's like around here; everywhere gets booked up in advance. The poor bloke would have been on the streets."

My face crumpled.

"And what with me now having both Emma *and* Josh to stay, even if I wanted it to, my place couldn't fit another body in."

My mind raced. It wasn't enough that my holiday of a lifetime had been ruined, my alternative staycation Christmas was about to follow suit. The universe had to be conspiring against me, because try as I might, I couldn't come up with another explanation.

"I'd hate to think of him on his own on Christmas Day and he'd be much more comfortable at yours."

I swallowed a whimper. What was Annie talking about? Fin couldn't stay at mine for Christmas. As nice as the man had proven himself, and as much as I liked him, the only things I really knew about Fin I'd read on the back of a book.

I pictured my staycation again. Me lounging on the sofa in my pyjamas, a mountain of festive snacks at the ready, all the while scrolling through the TV channels for festive movies. I imagined drinking copious amounts of wine and tackling my humongous to-be-read pile of books. I envisaged writing my long-term to-do wish list, as I reflected on my past and planned for my future. What I didn't see in my mind's eye was Fin.

"And no doubt very appreciative," Annie added.

I didn't want appreciation, I wanted solitude.

"Thank you, Holly," Annie said. "You don't know how much this means to me. I might not have seen Fin for years, but I'd have hated having to let him down." Annie's loyalty was touching. She'd been a dependable and steadfast friend to me, so it came as no surprise that she was the same with Fin. He might have been her husband's cousin, but I knew that to Annie that made him her family too.

"No problem," I said, my voice jumping an octave.

Annie giggled. "I'm meeting him for lunch. I can't wait to tell him. He'll be as thrilled as I am."

Standing there, I told myself at least someone was.

18

———

Landing home, I grabbed the Secret Santa I'd been gifted at work, dreading to think what it might be. If there was a world record for buying the most random gifts ever, my colleagues would win hands down. Looking at it, I told myself there was no point trying to guess and stuffing it into my bag, I climbed out of the car.

Tired and fed up I dragged my feet as I made my way to the house. I paused as I clocked a couple of teenage girls opposite with mobile phones in their hands. It was far too cold for anyone to be out doing nothing and I narrowed my eyes, wondering if they were there to catch a glimpse of Fin. That was all I needed. Seeing me stare at them, suspicious, they giggled before scarpering off down the street, making me wonder if I was simply being paranoid. I shook my head. While I'd hoped for a Christmas to remember, that year's was turning out to be memorable for all the wrong reasons, and instead of feeling any yuletide spirit, I felt sorry for myself.

With my last shift before Christmas complete, I should have been racing inside for a quick shower, before grabbing my suitcase and jumping into a taxi headed for the airport hotel. I should have been flying off into the sun the following day, enjoying ten days of me-time, relaxing, having fun, and thinking about my future. As it was, I couldn't even look forward to the alternative plan of locking the front door behind me, with nothing but ten days of blissful hibernation ahead. I ruined that for myself when I agreed to provide board and lodgings to a well-known homeless chef; a chef that Annie insisted liked me.

I wished she hadn't. The last few days had been complicated enough.

I sighed again as I thought about the day's events. Knowing I only had myself to blame, I mocked my own stupidity. *Whatever it is, it's a yes from me...* I ridiculed. *See it as a gift, to celebrate becoming a grandparent...* I shook my head once more, wondering why I couldn't have kept my big mouth shut.

I paused to gather myself before entering. Despite my self-pity, I knew it wouldn't be fair on Fin if I spent the whole evening sulking. None of what had happened was his fault. I moved to let myself in.

"Jesus Christ!" I shrieked, convinced my heart had burst. Before my hand had even touched the handle, the door flew open.

"Close your eyes," Fin said, suddenly appearing. He'd clearly been waiting to accost me.

Too busy trying not to have a coronary to follow his instruction, I put my hand up to my chest, telling myself to breathe. "Are you trying to kill me?" I asked.

Fin laughed. "Death by shut-eye. That's a new one on me."

Struggling to match his good humour, I flashed Fin a dirty look.

"Come on, Holly. Play along."

"Why? What have you done?" I took in Fin's childlike

demeanour. As if shocking me into a heart attack wasn't enough, he obviously had another surprise ready for me. The way my day was going I dreaded to think what lay in store. I tried to look over Fin's shoulder for a glimpse, but not only was he too tall for that, he shifted his position making it even more impossible for me to see. "Fin, please. It's been a long day."

He tilted his head, giving me what were, no doubt, his best puppy-dog eyes and looking at him, it was clear that if I ever wanted to get back inside my own house I'd have to do as he asked. My shoulders slumped. "This had better be good," I said. In danger of sounding like a stroppy teenager, I reminded myself that Fin was as stuck with me as was I with him.

His palm was warm as he took my hand, and liking the feel of his firm grip, I let him guide me over the threshold and into the house. I heard the door close behind us before he led me partway down the hall. He brought me to a stop before steering me to the right and I knew we were entering the lounge.

"Ready?" he asked, bringing me to a final standstill.

"As I'll ever be," I replied.

He let go of me and I sensed him take a step back. "Open your eyes," he said.

Again, I did as I was told, my eyes widening at the sight that greeted me. "Oh, Fin," I said, suddenly overcome. "But how?" The smell of pine needles permeated the air, courtesy of the huge tree sitting pride of place in the window. Appreciating the man's efforts, I couldn't help but smile. "You did all this for me?"

More kitsch than co-ordinated, the tree wasn't what some would call tasteful in the decoration department. There was no scheme or order to it, just a riot of every colour imaginable. Blue baubles hung next to red baubles, green baubles, purple and pink, all of them different in shape and size. Gold and silver tinsel intertwined as each length flowed from top to bottom like a pair of glittery helter-skelters. Candy canes and nets of chocolate coins fought for attention amongst the chaos, and Christmas crackers lay precariously on most of the tree's branches. The whole ensemble was a colourful, hot mess, yet at the same time the most wonderful sight.

"I know it's not the tidiest of trees," Fin said. "But it's better than no tree at all."

"I think it's perfect," I replied, touched by the work he'd put in. "I love it."

Fin put his arm around my shoulders, and we both simply stood there appreciating his handiwork. I leaned into him and rested my head against his chest. I breathed in his scent, happy to enjoy the moment. A stark contrast to when I'd first met Fin, I realised. Back then my body had stiffened at his touch.

"Annie carted everything up from town," Fin said. "But I did all the decorating."

I smiled, making a mental note to ring and thank her. "That was kind," I said.

"It was meant to be my leaving present to say thanks for having me." Fin looked down at me, his eyes sparkling. "But now we get to enjoy it together."

I smiled back at him, in that moment unable to think of anything better.

"Oh, before I forget." Fin let go of my shoulder, raced over to the sofa and pulled something from behind a cushion. "For you."

I laughed as he held out the funniest looking Christmas tree angel I'd ever had the pleasure of seeing. It had boggly eyes and a wonky halo, which for some inexplicable reason made it even more adorable. "Thank you," I said, taking it from him. I watched him pick up my huge heavy square pouffe and carry it over to the tree – and with such ease, I noted.

"Go on then," he said, gesturing me to stand on it.

I smiled in delight as I took his hand and stepped up onto

the pouffe. I found myself forced to stretch more than was comfortable as I put the angel where she belonged on top of the tree. "Gorgeous," I said, at last stepping down to admire her.

"We're not quite finished yet," Fin said.

"You mean there's more?"

He reached down and as I heard the flip of a switch the tree suddenly sprang to life. An assortment of colourful fairy lights flashed amongst the rest of the tree's finery, making the baubles and tinsel glisten all the more.

"This is wonderful," I said. "Thank you."

"It's not just to show my appreciation. As you were meant to be going on holiday tomorrow," Fin said. "I thought you might need cheering up. Plus, as we're going to be spending Christmas together, I wanted to make the most of it." As he looked at me, his eyes seemed to question mine.

"I couldn't agree more," I replied.

"Ooh," Fin said, the moment gone as he suddenly seemed to remember something. "You'll never guess what else I got." He stepped back out into the hall. "Come on," he said.

I followed him to the kitchen curious as to what could cause such added excitement.

"Ta da!" he said, throwing his arms out wide in celebration of the dining table. "How much fun are we going to have?"

I let out a laugh, finding myself cast back to mine and Vee's childhood and the hours we'd spent handmaking decorations. "We're putting together our own paper chains, I see." I took in the sheets of colourful paper, the scissors to cut the sheets into strips, and the couple of glue sticks awaiting mine and Fin's attention.

"We most certainly are." Fin indicated the oven, before looking straight at me. "What else are we going to do while we wait for the casserole to finish cooking?"

I willed myself not to blush as butterflies fluttered in my

tummy. Knowing exactly what else we could have been doing, I questioned whether the twinkle in his eye meant Fin was thinking the same as me. My heart skipped a beat as we stared at each other. Had Annie been right earlier? Did Fin like *like* me?

The doorbell rang, before I got an answer to either question.

19

"Shit!" I said, as my eyes darted towards the front door and then to Fin. "Who could that be?"

Whoever it was knocked again.

"I'm supposed to be on my way to the airport by now," I said, "Everyone knows that." Feeling panicked, I heard someone try the handle, before the front door opened completely. My heart raced at the prospect of it being Mum and Dad. "They're letting themselves in. What shall I do?"

"Yoo-hoo!" a female voice called out.

"Roberta!" I said. "What's she doing here?" Speaking in hushed tones, I couldn't believe she'd entered my house uninvited. Not only that, if she saw me, she was bound to tell the world I hadn't gone to the Caribbean. I scanned the room looking for a hiding place, but apart from under the table which I'd never get away with, I couldn't see anywhere. I danced about, desperate, as my eyes searched, but my mind refused to focus.

"It's only me," Roberta said. The sound of her stilettos got closer as she made her way down the hall.

"Quick!" Fin said, in a frantic whisper. "In here." He leapt towards the tallest cupboard in the kitchen, opening the door to the only space just about big enough to house an ironing board and vacuum in my small cottage. He grabbed them and pulled them out to make room for me. "In here."

I squealed at the suggestion, struggling to accept I was having to conceal myself into such a tight space. "Please tell me you're joking?" I said. However, with no time to argue, I scowled and did as I was told. Squeezing in, I lowered into a sitting position as Fin closed the door again and shut me away. *Not so big-boned now, are you?* I silently asked. Trying to think positive, I was surprised I could fit into any cupboard at all.

"Fin, are you there?" I heard Roberta ask as she clearly entered the room. "I saw the lights on and thought I'd come say hello."

I glowered, realising what the woman was up to. Thinking I was on my way to the Caribbean, she was seizing the opportunity to get closer to Fin. I looked down at my attire as I pictured her, all dressed up with perfect hair and make-up. Ready to reel the man in and desperate for attention, she probably had the local papers on speed dial.

"Oh," she said, sounding surprised. "Holly's got you doing a spring clean while she's away, has she?"

Hearing Roberta's not so subtle dig, I narrowed my eyes, silently cursing her in the knowledge that I couldn't respond. When it came to me, Roberta had never been able to resist making some sort of personal attack and undermining me in front of Fin was, no doubt, part of her game plan. I imagined her casting a critical eye over the rest of the room for more ammunition to throw at me. Having never been in my house before, I knew she'd be stood there, with her poker-straight hair and bright red lipstick, eagerly taking everything in.

"As well as making Christmas decorations, I see," Roberta said, proving my point. "She is keeping you busy."

"You know Holly," Fin replied, his voice upbeat. "She does like to let everyone know who's boss."

Listening to the humour in his voice, my eyes widened, as I wondered if his comment was for my benefit. But while Fin might have thought he was being funny, the last person he should've been saying things like that to was Roberta. Whether Fin joked or not, Roberta would choose to take his comment literally, giving her yet another reason to dislike me.

"Yes, I've heard that about her," she replied.

I clamped down on my jaw and pursed my lips, resisting the need to respond as she again proved my point.

Sitting there, my bum began to ache as I questioned why the woman seemed to disapprove of my existence. I knew it had nothing to do with me as an individual. After all, how could it? The two of us were relative strangers. Other than strained politeness, we barely spoke to each other let alone mingled. I scowled, failing to care what Roberta thought of me one way or the other.

"Not how I like to treat *my* guests," Roberta said, her tone inviting.

I silently scoffed. *I'll bet.*

"I can imagine," Fin replied, his tone flat.

Good response.

"How can I help you?"

I smiled to myself. It was heart-warming to think women like Roberta had no impact on Fin. Although being a rather handsome chap *and* a TV star, both in the UK and the US, he was probably used to women throwing themselves at him. After a while, I supposed behaviour like that got boring. Under those circumstances, I thought it no wonder he'd kept his career quiet.

"You're not going to believe this..." Roberta said, her voice sickly sweet.

I rolled my eyes. Whatever she was about to say I knew I certainly wouldn't.

"But I've run out of sugar."

"Sugar?" Fin asked.

I stifled a giggle, pleased to hear he wasn't having a word of it either.

"I'm afraid so." She paused, no doubt, to flutter her eyelashes. "I wondered if I could borrow some."

No, you damn well can't.

"Yeah, sure," Fin replied, much to my frustration.

I heard Fin open a cupboard door, followed by the chink of crockery as he obviously reached for a cup. I heard paper packaging being opened, the swooshing of granules being poured, and to my annoyance, stiletto heels clip-clopping on the stone floor as Roberta stepped further into the room. My back began to ache and careful not to make any noise, I brought my knees higher up to my chest, hoping that might stretch my spine out a little. Feeling increasingly uncomfortable, I willed Fin to tell her to take her sugar and bugger off home.

"A teabag and some hot water to go with a spoonful of that would be nice," Roberta said.

Surprised to hear the tap running, I turned my head their way. *Please tell me you're not filling the kettle.* Forced to ask what Fin thought he was doing, I was ready for bursting out of my hiding place.

"Just so you know," Roberta said.

Here we go, I thought, to the sound of her stilettos edging closer still. *She's going in for the kill.*

"My offer still stands."

I knew it.

"Offer?" Fin replied.

"To show you around some of the sights. Now Holly's away I thought we could..."

She let her sentence trail off, but the inference was there and interested to know how Fin might respond, I resisted the urge to burst out of the cupboard and tell her where to go. Instead, I waited for him to speak, at the same time thinking about my new mattress, praying to God I wouldn't have to buy yet another one.

"Well there's no point sitting around here on your own. Not when you could be having fun with me."

I pictured Roberta's accompanying smile, wanting nothing more than to wipe it clean off.

"I'll bear that in mind," Fin said, demonstrating absolutely no interest whatsoever.

Sitting there in my cubbyhole, I felt like cheering.

"So what brings you to the Dales?" she asked, clearly refusing to get the message. "A new work project by any chance?"

"Oh, you know," Fin replied, to the sound of cups chinking.

I shook my head, unable to believe he was really going to sit down for a cup of tea and a chat, all the while knowing I was stuck in a cupboard.

"I get it," Roberta said. "You can't talk about it. It's all hush hush."

"Not as far as I'm concerned," Fin replied, his confidence on the matter apparent.

"Really?" Roberta said, coming over all excited.

Really? I thought. Just like my neighbour, I was keen to hear more.

"In that case, please do tell."

Yes, please do.

I listened to the sound of hot water pouring, shortly followed by what I assumed was a spoon tinkling against the inside of the teapot as Fin stirred. The fridge door opened. "Milk?" Fin asked. The man was obviously playing with one or both of us.

"Just a splash," she said. She seemed to pause before speaking again. "You were saying..."

Fin got back to the subject at hand. "Well the thing is..."

"Yes?"

"I'm mean, I'm not sure I should *really* be telling you anything. Although *I* don't mind sharing, of course..."

"Of course." Like me, the woman clearly hung on Fin's every word.

"But I have to think about the other party involved."

"Other party?"

Wondering where Fin was taking their conversation, my interest was piqued as much as Roberta's. And just as Roberta hoped he was about to disclose some top-secret work project, I realised I did too. Whatever it was Fin was about to say, I willed him to spit it out.

"I'm talking about Holly."

"Holly?"

Me? I jerked my head in his general direction. *What did I have to do with anything?*

"You know how private she is," Fin continued. "So, if word was to get out that we're... you know?"

That we're... you know, what? Suddenly horrified, it dawned on me what Fin was implying. *Please don't do this...*

"You're not suggesting...? You mean you and Holly are...?"

"Yes," Fin said, loud and clear. "We most definitely are."

I put a hand over my mouth to stop myself from shrieking. While Fin hadn't said anything explicit, he'd said enough to set the local tongues wagging. Sat cooped up in that cupboard, I was powerless to deny it. I had to wonder if the man had gone mad.

"I see," Roberta said. "Well I wasn't expecting that."

Neither was I.

I narrowed my eyes to the sound of her stilettos suddenly on the move again.

"You're leaving?" Fin asked. "So soon?" The man was evidently smirking. "But what about your tea?"

"Keep it," Roberta replied.

Again, I put a hand over my mouth. This time to stop myself from laughing. While it served the woman right, I didn't think I'd ever heard Roberta so displeased.

"I prefer coffee anyway," she said.

I sat silent, waiting until I heard the front door open and slam shut, before breaking out of my hiding place. Landing on my knees, I struggled to get up. "You do know what you've just done, don't you?" I asked, at the same time grabbing at the kitchen worktop to haul myself onto my feet. "She'll make one of us pay for this."

He laughed. "Pay for what?"

"The fact that you turned down her advances."

"Please tell me you didn't expect anything different?"

I shifted on my feet. "Of course not."

"Then what's the problem?"

"I'm just worried that..." It wasn't me I was concerned about. Being a nobody, I didn't have any reputation to lose. At least not of the positive kind if Roberta had anything to do with things. However, when it came to Fin and his reputation, one that he had to have worked hard for, it was a different story altogether. "I'm thinking of you," I said.

Fin's expression softened. "Does it matter if people think we're in a relationship?"

"But we're not."

"That doesn't answer my question."

While Fin stood there, one eyebrow raised, waiting for a response, I looked around for a diversion. "We don't have time to mess about with the hypothetical, Fin," I said, indicating the table. "We still have paper chains to make."

20

A mountain of paper chains sat on one side of the table, while Fin and I sat at the other finishing off the tasty casserole Fin had made. "That was delicious," I said, placing my spoon down on my empty plate. With my stomach feeling fit to burst, I leaned back in my seat. "I couldn't eat another thing."

"Don't get too comfortable," Fin replied. He indicated the home-made Christmas decorations. "We've still got to hang that lot yet."

I groaned at the prospect, telling myself that the food I'd just eaten needed to do a whole lot of settling before I could even think about getting on with a task like that. I rose to my feet and picked up our plates. The washing up was the least I could do after all of Fin's hard work.

Heading for the sink, I placed everything down on the counter and decided the dishes could wait a bit longer. "More wine?" I asked, instead. I didn't wait for Fin's answer, I simply reached for the bottle. Having put the Roberta debacle behind me I had had the most wonderful carefree evening reminiscent of my childhood and I wanted to hold on to my contentment for as long as I could.

In the darkness outside something caught the corner of my eye. "What's that?" I asked. I turned to Fin, before looking out into the garden. I suddenly freaked and the wine bottle slipped from my hand.

Fin jumped to his feet as it smashed to smithereens. "What is it?" he said, racing over.

"There was a face." I pointed to the window. "Someone's out there." A picture of Roberta popped into my head, followed by images of the paparazzi hiding in bushes. My heart raced. I wouldn't have put it past her to call them. Having been rebuffed, she'd have done anything to ruin my happiness. Calling in the press was probably her way of ensuring Fin was long gone by the time I got back off my alleged holiday. *Oh, Lordy*, I thought, *I should have got rid of Fin no matter what.*

"You stay here," he said, ready to go and investigate.

My panic continued. The media loved knocking celebrities down. Newspapers were full of headlines depicting how far the paparazzi went to get the perfect photo. And by "perfect" they meant photos which showed people like Fin in a bad light. "Be careful," I said, but before Fin got the chance to find out who was out there, the back door flew open.

I screamed, before looking for something to grab.

Fin froze as he stared at the intruder.

I froze, too, wooden spoon raised high. "Vee!" I said, shocked to see she was the trespasser, not the man with a camera I had been expecting.

"Who else would it be?" she asked.

I lowered my arm. "What are you playing at? You scared me half to death."

Fin looked from her to me, clearly confused. "You two know each other?"

"Yes," I replied, trying to control my heartbeat. "This is my sister."

"Not that you'd know it," Vee said, glaring at me.

I stared back, wondering why suddenly everyone thought they could let themselves into my house uninvited. "I don't know if it's a full moon out there, but people seem to be acting very strangely tonight."

Mitch suddenly appeared in the doorway behind Vee. He panted, trying to catch his breath. He'd obviously ran to catch up with her, no doubt parking the car while she raced on ahead. "Sorry," he said. "I did try to get her to call, but she wasn't having it." He spotted Fin. "Oh, hi there. I'm Mitch, Holly's brother-in-law."

Fin nodded in acknowledgement, before looking to me, eyebrows raised, clearly wondering what was going on. I shrugged. As much in the dark as him, I wished I knew.

Mitch took a step forward, opening his mouth to speak, but my sister put a hand up to silence him.

"Don't you dare say this is my hormones," Vee said to her husband. "I mean it. If you quote one more pregnancy book, or try to mansplain my own body to me, I swear I will swing for you."

Mitch did as he was told and stepped back again, while Vee returned her attention to me. "Why would Holly go food shopping, I ask myself," my sister said. "If she's not going to be around to eat anything?"

Recalling my midnight supermarket run, I tried but failed to recall seeing anyone that Vee might know. My nerves crept to the fore and I let out a hollow laugh. "Who said I've been shopping?" I asked, faking innocence.

Vee scoffed. "There's no point denying it. Elizabeth's cousin's niece's best friend saw you."

Fin's face contorted.

"What can I say?" I said to him. "It's the Yorkshire Dales. Everyone knows everyone."

"Don't change the subject," Vee said.

I suddenly frowned, my eyes narrowing as I turned my attention back at Vee. "Hang on a minute. You're telling me that Elizabeth's cousin's niece's best friend is Jeremy's bit on the side?" Again, I looked at Fin. "Don't ask."

"What does it matter?" Vee replied. "I'm more interested in what you're still doing here. Shouldn't you be at some hotel by now?" She turned to Fin. "And pray tell, who are you?"

Please don't recognise him, please don't recognise him, I repeated over and over. The way things were going, that would be one problem too many.

"Fin," he replied. He smiled, holding out a hand to formally introduce himself but much to my embarrassment Vee glared in response. Fin let his hand drop, before looking to Mitch, who simply shrugged his shoulders, his face full of sympathy.

"Fin's a guest," I said. "He's staying with me for a while."

"Since when?" Vee asked.

"It's a long story."

"I've got time."

I didn't respond.

"And your holiday?" Vee asked. "What happened to that?"

I felt like a naughty schoolgirl in trouble with the headmistress. "It got cancelled. Without my knowledge."

"Why didn't you tell me?" She turned to Fin again, with a look of disdain. "Because of you, I suppose. Who are you anyway? And what are you doing here?"

"Hey, Vee. Come on," I said. Pregnant or not, my sister was going too far and I needed to pull her into line. "I don't know what's got into you, but none of this is his fault." I took a deep breath, resigned to telling the truth. "I didn't mention my holiday being cancelled because there was no need to. I'm still not going to Mum and Dad's. I've decided to have a staycation instead."

Vee frowned. "A what?"

Fin stepped forward. "It's when instead of–"

Vee flashed him a look, enough to silence his explanation. "I need to sit down," she suddenly said.

"I'll go and clean that glass up, shall I?" Fin asked.

"Please," I replied, grateful.

"I'll put the kettle on," Mitch said, following him over.

With the two of them out of the way, I joined Vee at the table.

"How could you do this to me?" she asked.

"Do what?"

"Leave me and Mitch to go to Mum and Dad's for Christmas without you there for support?" She put her hand on her belly.

"What do you mean, for support?"

"We'll need you as a distraction. You do know Mum's taken to calling the baby JC? For Jesus Christ?"

I looked over to my brother-in-law for confirmation. After all, the mood Vee was in, she could easily have made that up. The man nodded, while I did my best not to smile at the news. "I didn't know that, no."

"Well she blooming well has. Come on, Holly, you have to be there. She'll be forcing me to eat laxatives or do star jumps. Mum will do anything to have a Christmas baby. I need you to divert the woman's attention. And if that doesn't work, to stop me from killing her."

"I think you're exaggerating there," I said. I knew Mum could be a bit off the wall and more than a tad Christmas obsessive, but no way would she try to induce her unborn grandchild just so she could have her own little baby Jesus.

Vee glared at me again. "It's just like you to stick up for her."

"Since when?" As far as I was concerned, Vee seemed to be going into the realms of fantasy.

I looked over at Fin and my brother-in-law. Fin appeared uncomfortable, although in his shoes I wouldn't know where to put myself either. Mitch, on the other hand, seemed at a loss. The situation we'd all found ourselves in clearly hadn't been covered in his pregnancy books. Catching their attention, I nodded to the door, my way of suggesting they might want to disappear for a while. Neither of them seemed to understand what I was saying, forcing me to jolt my head even harder. I rolled my eyes at their apparent stupidity. "Fin, why don't you and Mitch hang some of these decorations?" I said, smiling. "You could even show Mitch the Christmas tree while you're at it."

At last, the penny seemed to drop.

"Oh, right," Fin said.

"No problem," Mitch said.

Fin fetched their drinks and grabbing a handful of the decorations we'd just made, led the way out into the hall.

Thank you, Mitch mouthed as he closed the door behind them.

"Do you want to tell me what's really going on here, Vee," I asked, glad to have the room to ourselves.

My sister looked at me, her expression desperate. "I'm scared, Holly."

"Of what?"

"Of not being good enough. As a parent, I mean. I know you don't believe me, but Mum will try something and what if it works? And if I can't protect my baby from my own mother, how am I going to keep him or her safe out there?" Vee gestured to the window and the world beyond.

As my heart went out to Vee, I took her hand. "It's exactly because you're thinking this way that you're going to make a great mum."

21

I stood at the sink with my hands submerged in water as I washed the dishes. Fin stood next to me with a tea towel drying them. We worked in silence. Vee's visit was clearly on his mind as much as it was on mine.

The earlier happy atmosphere had all but evaporated thanks to my sister. Pregnant or not, she had no right to sneak around the garden trying to catch me out before bursting in and demanding answers to her questions. I felt embarrassed at the way she spoke to Fin; at the way she accused him of being the reason I wasn't on holiday. At thirty-three years old I'd earnt the right to decide how I spent my time and with whom.

Not that anyone would think so. Even I saw the contradiction in the way I had to sneak around.

I also felt sad. Vee was obviously worried about the responsibility that came with parenthood. So much so it was making her irrational.

But I hadn't allowed myself to be bullied. Much to my sister's exasperation, I stuck to my word about not going to our parents for Christmas. Then again, she stuck to her insistence that I should.

However, to be fair, Vee had promised not to drop me in it with our parents. She'd agreed to keep the news about both my cancelled holiday and staycation to herself.

I snuck a glance at Fin, wondering what he must be thinking. As introductions go, Vee can't have made a good first impression. In my defence though, I had already hinted that my family weren't what most would call normal. The Noelles didn't do things by halves.

"You okay?" Fin asked. He put a hand on my arm as he spoke.

I nodded, but I could see he didn't believe me. I thought about my kind, caring and placid sister. "It's just not like Vee to be so angry," I said. "I've never known her to be so unreasonable. It's like she's been taken over."

"That's pregnancy for you."

I frowned. "Well if that's what it does, I'm glad I'll never experience it."

"You don't want children?" Fin asked.

I let out a laugh. "Chance would be a fine thing. It takes two remember."

"It certainly does," Fin replied, giving me one of his winks.

A tingle ran up my spine, but I ignored it, telling myself that Fin was just being Fin, teasing me as usual.

"Honestly, I wouldn't worry about your sister," Fin said. "Having a baby can do weird and wonderful things to a woman's body and mind."

He was beginning to sound like Mitch. "And you'd know this how?" I asked.

"A friend of mine's wife went practically doolally during her latter stages. One minute she'd be laughing, in the next she'd be yelling, and in the next she'd be crying. I don't know how the rest of the family kept up."

I knew he was exaggerating for my benefit. After all, there were mood swings and there were mood swings.

"But I wouldn't worry. Whatever is going on with your sister, things will settle down again. After the birth she'll be back to normal."

"How can you be so understanding?" I asked. "After the way she treated you, the things she said." My family members had been known to embarrass me over the years, but that night Vee had taken things to a whole new level.

"I've had worse," Fin replied. "Your sister's a kitten compared to some of the chefs I've worked under."

I smiled.

"That's better," he said, getting back to his drying up. Picking up a plate, he paused. "Why don't you give your mum a ring? Gauge if there's any truth to Vee's worries?"

"You think I should?"

"It might put your mind at rest, even if it won't Vee's."

"I think I will," I replied, drying my hands on the corner of the tea towel Fin was using. "And thank you."

"For what?"

"For being you."

I collected my phone off the dining table and went through to the lounge. I smiled at the Christmas tree as I entered, allowing myself a moment of joy. But my happiness was soon replaced with anxiety. Scrolling for my parents' number, I clicked call, at the same time praying that Vee was wrong, that Mum wasn't hell-bent on having a Christmas grandchild. Not that I planned on asking Mum outright if she was intent on forcing Vee into labour.

"Hello," Dad said, answering my call.

"Hi, Dad," I said, surprised to hear his voice rather than Mum's. More often than not, she was the one to pick up.

"Holly," he replied. "I'm so pleased you rang. You got to the hotel all right, then?"

"Er, yes, I did," I said. Thanks to Vee's extraordinary visit, I'd forgotten that that was where I was supposed to be, and Dad's reminder caught me off guard.

"Not too far from the terminal, is it?"

"No," I said. "Easily walking distance."

"That's good. Now make sure you set your alarm for the morning. You don't want to be sleeping in if you can help it."

I smiled. "I'll set my alarm, Dad."

"And you've got your passport and boarding card?"

"I have."

"I'm just checking. You want to be able to get on that plane. And you're not carrying anything for anyone else, are you?"

I rolled my eyes. "No, Dad."

"Good. Because goodness knows how much trouble that would get you into. What about liquids? Nothing over a hundred millilitres in your hand luggage?"

"Again, Dad, that would be a no." I paused, frowning as I considered the information being requested. "Dad?"

"Yes, love."

"These questions of yours, are they written down by any chance?"

"They are. On a list your Mum put together. Why?"

"Because I have travelled before, you know. I'm aware of all the dos and don'ts."

"Not to somewhere as far away as the Caribbean, you haven't. And besides, there's nothing wrong with a bit of reassurance. You're travelling on your own, which is enough for us to be thinking about, without all these added concerns."

Listening to Dad, I felt terrible. There he and Mum were, scared for my safety and all for no reason. I was almost tempted to head to the airport and jump on a plane for real regardless of its destination, simply to give credence to what my parents were going through. "Okay," I replied. "I understand, ask away."

"I think that's it," Dad said. "Mum can message you if she thinks of anymore."

"Speaking of Mum," I said, acknowledging the fact that she was unusually quiet. After making it her mission to prevent me from going anywhere over Christmas, I'd expected at least some fighting talk from her corner. "Is she there?"

"She's not, no."

"Really?"

"She had to go out."

That was a surprise. "You told her I was ringing from the airport hotel, though, didn't you? When I mentioned it the other day?"

"I did."

I grimaced, wondering what could be so important that she wouldn't be around to take my call. Mum had created such a fuss over my holiday and for her to miss out on a last-ditch attempt at getting me to stay seemed odd.

"There's been some sort of emergency," Dad said.

"What kind of an emergency?"

"Something to do with Joyce."

"Joyce from Zumba."

"How should I know where the woman hails from."

I felt too slighted to explain to Dad that Zumba was a form of exercise, not the name of a town. How could Mum let Joyce take priority over me, her daughter?

"Or it could have been Wendy," Dad continued.

"Wendy from the dominoes group?" I asked, not that it mattered, Mum had still put someone else first.

"To be honest, I haven't a clue who it is. Your Mum's in touch with so many people it's hard to keep up."

My anxiety grew as I wondered if Dad hadn't listened or if

something else was at play. Although to be fair, Mum did have a wide circle of friends and she was always mentioning someone or other.

I thought back to previous conversations I'd had with Mum, unable to recall her highlighting any issues amongst anyone she knew, and Mum did like to keep me up-to-date with local comings and goings. Mum wasn't salacious or gossipy like some, she was simply a typical Yorkshire Dales woman who assumed everyone knew everyone and would, therefore, care about what was happening in their lives. Although in my case, she couldn't have been more wrong. I had no interest.

"You know me," Dad said. "I just let your Mum do what she needs to do. Anyway, I should let you go." He suddenly seemed in a rush to get rid of me. "You'll be wanting to get some sleep before that long flight tomorrow."

"Everything is all right, isn't it, Dad?" I asked, concerned.

"What do you mean?"

"I'm just surprised Mum isn't around after all the noise she made."

Dad sighed.

"Dad, what's going on?"

"If I'm honest, Holly, I don't think there's any emergency at all."

"But a second ago you said there was."

"I think your Mum made it up as an excuse to go out."

"But why would she do that?" I asked, becoming more perplexed by the minute. "Doesn't she want to talk to me?"

"It's not that, Holly. I think it's her way of holding on to her belief that you'll be around for Christmas."

Listening to Dad, I didn't know whether to laugh or cry. "Well she's in for one hell of a shock Christmas morning then," I said, starting to feel affronted. Wondering what was wrong with my family, I could only assume Mum was living in the same fantasy land as Vee.

"Let me deal with your Mum," Dad said. "You just go and enjoy your holiday. It's the least you deserve. Don't forget to ring when you get there though."

"I won't," I said, hating lying to the man. Ending the call, I sat pensive, mulling over his suggestion that Mum might be holding on to some misguided belief. I'd made it more than clear they were celebrating without me that year. In fact, I couldn't have made it any clearer.

"Everything okay?" Fin popped his head into the room.

I scoffed. "I haven't a clue."

He stepped into full view and approaching, handed me a mug. "I thought you might want one of these." He smiled. "Baileys and hot chocolate?"

"Very Christmassy," I said, trying to lift my spirits.

Fin took the seat next to me. "I'm here if you want to talk, you know."

"Thank you," I replied, appreciating his kind offer. But all the appreciation in the world couldn't alter the fact that my whole family was just plain bonkers.

22

THREE DAYS UNTIL CHRISTMAS

Determined to start my staycation as I meant to go on, I put all thoughts of Vee, Mum and Dad to the back of my mind. I told myself they were grown adults and that whatever issues they had going on in their crazy little worlds, they could sort them all out without any interference from me. As for my cancelled holiday, I might not have been sunning myself in paradise, but as far as I was concerned, that didn't mean I couldn't relax and make the most of my Christmas break.

For the first time since Fin's arrival I had the whole house to myself. He'd needed to go to Leeds, something to do with work. However, no additional information was forthcoming and I didn't push. I'd accepted the fact that he wasn't going to share the more glittering side of his career with me. Fin planned on taking the train, but knowing our local network I didn't think it worth the risk. Not the most reliable of services, a leaf on the track was enough to cause a delay and with snow forecast, it was odds on Fin would end up stranded.

"I'll be fine," he said, dismissive, when I offered him the use of my car.

However, a quick call to the insurance company and I was handing him the keys.

Fresh out of the shower and wearing a brand-new pair of pyjamas, I smiled, content with a bag of popcorn in hand, and entered the lounge. I grabbed the TV remote and plonked myself down on the sofa ready to put my feet up and veg the day away. "Now for a bit of me-time," I said.

Switching on the telly I scrolled through the channels, my enthusiasm waning as I took in the range of viewing choice. An hour-long news programme, a fly-on-the-wall courtroom reality show, re-runs of old soap operas, the list went on. A World War Two documentary, an in-depth profile of the royal family... There had to be a happy uplifting Christmas movie somewhere. As I carried on channel hopping, it appeared not, and disappointed, I switched off the TV altogether. "Well that's that," I said, having found nothing at all of interest.

I sat in the silence, one leg crossed over the other, my foot swinging left to right. Glancing over at the bookcase, I supposed I could read, but I didn't really feel in the mood. *Ten whole days*, I told myself. *No work, no drama, no fuss.* I looked around the room, before my eyes settled on the window and the street beyond.

I found myself wondering what Fin was up to and what time he might be back. I'd obviously got used to having him around as the place was a bit too quiet without him. I pictured Fin enjoying a coffee at some city centre street café, browsing the shops, or visiting a gallery and I felt jealous.

I'd been looking forward to doing nothing, but it wasn't half boring.

Unless... I thought, a mischievous smile spreading across my face.

I turned the television back on and feeling naughty for doing so, began searching through its catch-up reality TV programming. My heart skipped a beat as I finally found the show I was interested in and staring at its title for a few seconds, I dared myself to press play. Diving into my bag of popcorn, I giggled to myself as Fin appeared on screen.

"I'm Finlay McCormack," he said, talking direct to the viewing public. "And this is *Cooking Hell.*"

My tummy tickled as I took in the man's gorgeousness. He looked every inch the professional in his chef whites. And hot, I had to admit, with his pushed back blond hair and Hollywood smile. The camera obviously liked Fin, which I guessed was one of the reasons why the programme had been such a roaring success. I sat back as the opening credits rolled, popping into my mouth one puffed out kernel of popcorn after another.

It appeared Fin wasn't the only host-come-judge, there were two more. One was an established food critic, Claudia Williams-Taylor, whom I'd never heard of. Although *once seen, never forgotten* sprang to mind thanks to her harsh words and peculiar dress sense. Her clashing outfits were as offensive as her mouth, and with one hurting people's eyes and the other people's pride, I was convinced both were responsible for the numerous tears amongst the contestants.

The final arbitrator didn't seem to have any culinary background at all. However, Jack Splat clearly loved his cuisine because whereas Claudia and Fin merely sampled the contestants' concoctions, Jack tended to clear everyone's plates. He didn't seem to have a bad word for any of the dishes put in front of him he just ate everything in sight. A stand-up comedian by profession, Jack was obviously there to balance out the intense competitive nature of the show with a few lighter moments.

While Fin and Claudia discussed food combinations, competitor progress, and whether the people taking part had what it took to be a professional chef or not, Jack's role seemed to be clock monitor and all-round good egg. He threw in the odd catch phrase, of course, "Winner, winner, chicken dinner," being just one of them.

Fin was the best of the three judges, in my opinion, and not because I was biased. Unlike Claudia who simply slated everything and Jack who didn't have anything other than "Ooh, that's delish!" to say, Fin offered constructive feedback on how dishes could be changed or tweaked to make them better, which the stressed-out contestants seemed to appreciate.

As I binged through the episodes, I saw a side to Fin I hadn't seen before. He had an air of authority, commanding respect from everyone around him. He was nothing at all like the casual fun-loving chef I'd got used to in my little kitchen and I had to admit I found this new-to-me persona of his very attractive. Plus the man clearly knew his stuff. Even I found Fin inspiring, despite having more in common with the stand-up comedian when it came to food.

I smiled a dirty smile, wondering whether if I asked Fin for cookery lessons he'd be just as stern with me.

Cooking Hell was one of those shows that featured a different set of participants each week, with only the winner of each set going through to the next round. Each episode began with the same lines.

"So we've met the contestants," Fin said.

"The knives are out," Claudia said.

"Let's start creating a stir," Jack said.

The end of each episode had a little ritual, too.

"So which contestant will be our winner?" Fin said.

"And who will be eating humble pie?" Claudia said.

"The person going through to the next round is..." Jack said.

Despite its cheesiness, the programme clearly had a winning formula and like the rest of the nation, I found myself hooked from the very first episode through to the last.

23

I sat, perched, on the edge of my seat full of anticipation. Having partaken in a *Cooking Hell* viewing marathon, I'd invested hours of time and energy in getting to that moment and I was eager to find out who the ultimate victor would be.

Taking in the final three contestants, I appreciated their nervousness. Round after round they had fought hard for their places in the final, conjuring up dishes, under the most extreme of circumstances and using some pretty weird and wonderful ingredients. Every plate had been worthy of attention in even the finest of restaurants. As they stood there, all holding hands as they waited for the winner to be announced, I had my fingers crossed for Daniel, a seriously talented home cook from Portsmouth.

My excitement began to build as I watched Fin prepare to speak. Never mind the competitors, the expectation was killing me.

"Time to find out who will be crowned *Cooking Hell's* king or queen," Fin said.

I let out a wistful sigh. Boy, was that man sexy.

Suddenly startled, I heard the front door open and close. Looking in the direction of the hall and then at the telly, I couldn't believe Fin chose that precise moment to land home. Talk about not-so-perfect timing, I was going to miss the winning reveal and shooting forward, I muttered expletives as I grabbed the TV remote and switched off the TV. As the screen went black, it seemed I'd been so engrossed in my viewing I hadn't realised the room had fallen into darkness. Taking advantage of the lack of light, I threw myself into a prone position, closed my eyes, and pretended to be having a nap.

"Are you asleep?" Fin asked, surprised, flipping the light on as he entered the room.

I screwed my eyes up as they struggled to acclimatise to the brightness. "What time is it?" I asked, my apparent awakening worthy of an Oscar.

Fin checked his watch. "Five o'clock."

"I may have been resting my eyes a little," I said. Fin laughed as I rose to my feet. Immediately needing to stretch out my back, *Cooking Hell* had obviously made me more tense than I'd realised. "Did you have a good day?"

"Productive. My work meeting went well."

"Anything interesting you'd like to share?" I said, hoping he'd finally open-up about his standing. Having, at last, seen his show for myself, I had tonnes of questions.

He looked at me as if he wanted to say something, but then seemed to change his mind. "Not really," he said instead, much to my disappointment. "Oh, and I called at Annie's on the way back."

I smiled as I recalled my friend's excitement at the prospect of becoming a grandmother. "How is she?"

"Clucking and fussing over her daughter like any mother hen."

I laughed, knowing that would suit Emma down to the ground. "That's a bit of a turnaround," I said. "Only days ago Annie was complaining about Emma not doing enough."

"Ah, but that was before she learned her daughter was carrying precious cargo," Fin replied. "Cup of tea?"

As he left the room, I paused to consider his words. He seemed to have a knack of saying the nicest of things. I knew if my friend hadn't told me, I'd never have guessed Fin was famous. Despite his Hollywood and UK connections, he didn't show off or name-drop or expect everyone to run around after him as if he was entitled. From what I saw, he didn't seem to have a *do you know who I am* bone in his body. I had no clue about the fortune, but Fin certainly had the fame, as well as the personality and good looks to go with it. I sighed, also picturing the calm, commanding and respected professional I'd just seen on TV. *No one's that perfect, surely?* I had to ask, before joining him in the kitchen.

"You'll never guess what I saw on my way back from Annie's," he said, as I sat at the table.

Taking in his sudden excitement, I guessed whatever it was had to be good.

"Only the most fantastic house ever." He brought our drinks over, taking the seat opposite.

"Really?" I asked, suddenly nervous.

"Talk about Christmas light crazy, the whole exterior was covered."

"On the way back from Annie's, you say?" My heart sank.

"And it didn't stop there. It had inflatable Santas and snowmen in the garden. There was even a giant sleigh on the roof."

"Sounds like you got a good look," I said, cringing.

"I certainly did."

Oh, Lordy.

"It was fantastic." Fin became more animated the more he talked. His hands gesticulated here, there, and everywhere as he described strings of icicles, flashing reindeer that appeared to dance, and a Father Christmas halfway down the chimney. "You couldn't count the number of bulbs in use," he said. "Thousands I'd say. I dread to think what the house's electricity bill comes in at." The man was clearly impressed. "And the number of people crowding outside, there had to be a charity box there somewhere."

"Oh, there is."

"So you know it?" Fin asked, evidently pleased to hear that.

I nodded. "Yes. I know it."

"I suppose you'd have to be blind not to, hey. Isn't it great?"

"It's something all right," I replied, not sure that was the word I'd have used to describe the house.

"And the commitment. Putting up those lights and taking them down has got to take, what? Six months?"

"At the very least."

"Honestly." Fin shook his head. "It's mental."

I picked up my tea and took a sip. "Isn't it," I said, unable to disagree. Knowing he was talking about Mum and Dad's house, Fin might not have been able to miss the extensive Christmas regalia, but I thanked goodness for small mercies, at least he hadn't clocked the car on their drive. A car so ugly and box-like they were bought and sold for next to nothing back in the day, on account of the more discerning driver preferring to be seen in something stylish.

"And what about the psyched-up Lada? What do you think that's all about?" Fin asked.

My heart sank. That was a question I'd been asking for years.

While Fin laughed, I squirmed. Out of all the times I'd wished I could claim to be adopted, that moment was up there in the top ten.

I thought back to the day Dad brought the damn thing home. Russian made and sky blue in colour, it resembled more of an underwater tank than it did a roadworthy car. In fact, Dad often joked about us all being safe if we were ever shot at when out and about. Not the most attractive of vehicles to start with, my father had to make it worse by adding red and white "go-faster stripes" as he called them. Down each side and up the bonnet to the windscreen, with a paintbrush, as if that excuse for a family vehicle didn't garner enough attention.

"As cars go, that one's got to be a classic," Fin continued. "If I hadn't been in such a rush to get back, I'd have stopped to have a proper look."

My ears pricked. "Why were you in a rush?" I asked, wondering what was so important. It wasn't as if I'd given him a curfew.

"Sorry?"

"To get back?"

He smiled, looking at me direct. "To see you, of course."

I came over all warm and fuzzy, at the same time telling myself not to take too much heed of Fin's words. The man was a tease, nothing more, nothing less.

He picked up his cup and got to his feet. "More tea?" he asked, seemingly oblivious to the effect his jokes were having.

I shook my head as he headed for the kettle.

"Holly, look!" Fin said. Staring out of the kitchen window, he frantically waved me over.

I jumped up from my seat to join him. "It's not Vee again, is it?" I asked, wondering what was going on out there.

Fin laughed. "Better than that. It's snowing."

As I stood at the window, I felt my face brighten at the sight. We both stared in awe as big fat snowflakes drifted from thick swollen clouds, the dense flurry covering rooftops, gardens, drystone walls and fields in a thick white blanket. "It's beginning to look a lot like Christmas," I said, happy to relish the weather in all its wintery glory. I'd always loved snow, as long as I could enjoy it from the warm confines of home.

Fin turned to look at me, a big grin spreading across his face. "Fancy a walk?" he asked.

24

"But I don't want to go out," I said, imagining all the cold and wet Fin wanted to subject me to.

Refusing to take no for an answer, he stood in front of me, with my coat in one hand and a pair of my boots in the other.

"And besides that, I can't leave the house. I'm supposed to be in the Caribbean remember?"

He continued to hold my things out ready for me to take.

"What if someone sees me?" I asked.

"They won't."

"They might," I said, to no avail. "And what if word gets back to Mum and Dad?"

"It won't."

With Fin still not budging on the matter, I looked down at my attire. "I'm not even dressed. I can't leave the house in my pyjamas."

"Have you seen how dark it is out there?"

I raised my eyebrows, unable to believe he would even consider me prancing about the streets in my nightwear an option.

"See it as your civic responsibility," he said, maintaining his stance. "To help out your fellow man."

I sighed. If I could see the constitutional stretch in that, he could too.

"Do you know how long it's been since I've experienced proper snow?" he asked.

I sighed, feeling myself waiver. My shoulders dropped. "Now I know how Mum felt," I said, recalling how I'd had an answer every time she pleaded with me not to go on holiday. "All right," I said. "I'll go for a walk."

Fin's face cracked into a smile.

"But I'm not going like this. You can at least let me get dressed." Leaving him to celebrate his victory, I stomped upstairs to get changed. I could feel the man's eyes on me as I went, readily imagining him craning his neck to ensure I wasn't about to lock myself in the bathroom. As tempting as that might have been, I headed straight to my wardrobe and pulled out a pair of jeans, before grabbing a T-shirt and a jumper from my chest of drawers. I grumbled to myself as I changed clothes, unable to help but envisage the tropical sunset that I was meant to be enjoying that evening. "This could not be any more different," I said, pulling on a pair of thick woolly socks.

Downstairs I found Fin already wrapped up and set to go. He passed me my boots so I could put them on. Then he held out my duffle coat so I could slip my arms in before he buttoned it up for me. He took my scarf from the bannister and wrapped it around my neck. I was happy to let him. In a weird way, his actions allowed me to think he cared.

"Ready?" Fin asked, once he'd trussed me up like a woollen chicken.

"As I'll ever be," I replied.

I locked the door behind us as we stepped outside, stuffing the key deep into my coat pocket. Turning left, we headed for the church with its historic stained-glass window that shone colourful and bright against the darkness, thanks to strategically placed interior lights. The air was fresh as I breathed and huge snowflakes continued to fall. Despite being soft, the blanket of white crunched underfoot and it was hard to work out where the pathway ended and the kerbside began.

"This is magical," Fin said, looking about him.

"It's certainly pretty," I replied. "*And romantic,*" I thought.

Fin stopped for a moment and finding myself a couple of steps ahead, I came to a halt too. I turned, taking in Fin's awe.

"I've missed this," he said, looking at the snowflakes all around him. "That sunshine you were after isn't all it's cracked up to be."

In spite of the cold, his wonder gave me a warm glow in my tummy. "I'll take your word for it," I said, at the same time indicating we move on. We followed the road past the pub, me keeping my head down lest one of its customers look out onto the street and clock me. Although I needn't have worried. As if sensing my concern, Fin moved from my left side to my right, blocking me from view and I smiled to myself, appreciating the gesture.

Continuing on our way, I spotted an empty field where snow lay perfect and undisturbed. I looked to Fin, wondering if he'd seen it as well. I smiled. After all, if I couldn't beat him, then it was only right I joined him. He had a glint in his eye, enough to tell me he had and that he, too, found the pristineness of the area too much of a temptation to resist.

"Snowman?" he said.

"Definitely," I replied, feeling like a naughty teenager.

My heart leapt at the touch of his hand taking mine as we raced over to the field gate. Sliding the lock to let ourselves in, we made sure to close it again behind us, laughing as we got straight to work.

"Put your back into it," Fin said, as what started as a tiny ball grew into a sphere so large it was hard to push, only for us to scoop up another handful of snow and repeat the process all over again.

We puffed and panted as we struggled to get the head on top of the body, before Fin took off his scarf and wrapped it around the snowman's neck. I searched for two fallen twigs long enough to be his arms, before we both stood back to admire our efforts.

"It's a shame we don't have anything for his face," I said.

"If he's still here tomorrow, I'll come back with a carrot and a couple of coals."

"I can't remember the last time I made one of these," I said, but it seemed Fin was already thinking about our next move.

"What about a snow angel? When was the last time you made one of those?" he asked.

I laughed. "You know, I can't remember that either."

Fin glanced round, looking for an area of the field we'd yet to spoil. "There's no time like the present," he said, identifying the perfect spot. "Race you!"

We both set off on a run, although admittedly, in my case it was more of a speed walk. Wading through snow had never been one of my strong points, so it came as no surprise to see Fin beat me to it.

He immediately threw himself down on the ground and began repeatedly sliding his arms and his legs in and out, as if doing a burst of horizontal star jumps.

I followed suit, giggling at my efforts. At thirty-three years old it was nice to remember what it was like to forget all responsibility in favour of *playing out*. Lying there, it was exhilarating. Eventually, my arms and legs grew tired and came to a stop. "You're going to have to help me up," I said to Fin, snowflakes landing on my face. "I'm not sure I can manage on my own."

He got to his feet, both of us laughing as he took my hands

and hauled me back onto mine. Our laughter faded and silence descended as we stood there simply staring at each other.

My heart began to race as I looked into Fin's eyes. Their intenseness was mesmerising and I couldn't bring myself to look away. I didn't care that my jeans were soaked through to my skin, or that my hands felt like ice, I could have stood there all night.

"Can I kiss you?" he asked, his gaze not moving either.

"Yes, please," I replied.

His hands wrapped around my waist. "You sure?"

I nodded. In that moment I wanted nothing more.

As Fin's face moved closer to mine, I couldn't deny the desire with which he looked at me. Butterflies played havoc in my tummy as I anticipated his lips touching mine and I closed my eyes in readiness, feeling his breath draw close. "Ouch!" I said, as something cold whacked me on the side of my head. I pulled back to the sound of cheering and laughter.

"Oi!" Fin called out.

Wondering what had just happened, I followed his sight line to a group of teenagers who, ready for battle, began pelting us with snowball after snowball.

Fin smiled and, happy to take them on, reached down to scoop up a ball of his own. "I'll cover you," Fin said, indicating the gate to the field. "Three, two, one. Go!"

I set off on a run towards safety, while Fin, grabbing handful after handful of snow, defended us both as best as he could. Of course, we were never going to win and by the time we got to the gate we were covered in white, both of us laughing at our ineptitude.

"Chickens!" one of the teenagers called out.

"Easy for them to say," Fin said. "They've got youth on their side."

"Speak for yourself," I replied, brushing myself down. "It's not that long ago since I was their age."

Fin took my hand with a smile. "I suppose we should head back and get out of these wet clothes."

We walked in silence, but there was no denying the air of expectancy that had built by the time we reached the house. Nervous, I dug in my pocket for the door key and my hand shook as I tried to get it in the lock.

"Let me," Fin said, and taking it from me, he let us both into the house.

The door closed behind us, but neither of us spoke as we took off our coats and boots. As we turned to look at each other, I knew I wanted Fin and going off his expression, I could see he wanted me in return. For the first time in I didn't know how long I felt beautiful and rather than wait for him to make the first move, I simply reached up and pulled his face towards mine. I moaned in pleasure as our lips merged and tongues entwined, our mouths only parting as we desperately pulled T-shirts and jumpers over each other's heads. Fin steered me towards the wall until my back pressed against it and as we kissed once more, one of his hands slid under my bra to caress my breast. With my body aching for more, my hand eagerly searched for Fin's jean zip and undoing it, I slid a hand inside the denim, feeling his penis, hard in my palm.

"Oh God," he said, taking a sharp intake of breath.

"Your room or mine?" I asked, desperate to feel him inside me.

The front door flew open and like two rabbits in headlights, Fin and I froze as we looked at each other.

"What the hell's going on here?" a voice said.

"Jesus, Mary and Joseph," said another.

Recognising who they belonged to I cringed, wanting the ground to swallow me whole. Fin's eyes drilled straight into mine. I could see he was trying not to giggle as he un-cupped my breast, while at the same time I discreetly pulled my hand out of his trousers.

We both slowly turned our faces towards the intruders and taking in their bright red jackets, thick black belts, and matching Santa hats, I knew Fin would be more surprised than me to find Mother and Father Christmas looking back.

"Mum, Dad," I said, trying to raise a welcoming smile. "What are you two doing here?"

25

With Mum and Dad safely ensconced at the kitchen dining table, Fin and I hastily put our clothes back on. I couldn't believe Mum and Dad had just burst in like that. Or that they knew I'd be home. I couldn't believe Vee would drop me in it when she'd promised to keep quiet.

"Well this is awkward," Fin said, stretching his T-shirt over his head. "And a little bit embarrassing."

"How do you think I feel?" I asked, keeping my voice down as I put my jumper on. "As if catching us at it isn't bad enough, the first time you meet my parents and they come dressed as a pair of Santa knock-offs!"

Fin held my gaze, biting down on his lips, before we both creased with laughter.

"It's not funny really," I said, trying to pull myself together.

"Oh, it is," Fin replied, as he tried to control his giggling.

"Ready?" I asked.

Fin zipped up his jeans.

I looked down at my own attire, checking I was also fully decent in the clothing department. I took a deep breath to compose myself before turning to leave, but Fin stopped me in my tracks.

"Hang on a minute," he said. Suddenly serious, Fin stepped towards me, cupped my cheeks with his hands, and pulled my face towards his.

As his lips met mine, I did nothing to resist his kiss, choosing instead to enjoy the moment.

"What are you doing out there?" Mum asked, cutting it short.

Fin pulled back and looked me in the eyes. "I am now," he whispered.

As Fin released his hold, I stood there for a second to gather myself. "Okay. Let's do this," I said, leading the way to the kitchen.

We entered to find Mum and Dad sat side by side, like two people waiting for a bus on their way home after a fancy-dress party. They stared straight ahead and taking in their blank expressions, I dreaded to think what was coming.

As if reading my thoughts, Fin put a comforting hand on my arm.

I smiled in response, appreciating the reassurance.

"Here you are," Dad said, he and Mum giving us their full attention.

"Cup of tea?" I asked. I headed for the kettle to set about making it, while Fin took the seat opposite Dad.

Glancing over at the three of them, Fin winked at me. He seemed surprisingly comfortable considering my parents had just surged in when he was about to have sex with their daughter. I busied myself, placing mugs, the milk jug, and a sugar bowl onto a tray, knowing if Mum had her way, this was the calm before the interrogation storm.

"Do I know you?" Mum asked Fin. "Have we met before?"

I'd expected her first round of questions to focus on why I wasn't in the Caribbean. Or why I was having sexual relations with a man who was, to them at least, a complete stranger. I looked over at the table, to see Mum scrutinising Fin's face and as I'd done with my sister when she had burst forth into my house, I prayed Mum wouldn't recognise him.

Fin smiled her way, but as much as he tried to hide it, her enquiry clearly unsettled him. "I don't think so," he replied, before looking at me as if to check I wasn't listening.

I diverted my gaze and pretending I wasn't, got back to making the tea.

"You look familiar," Mum continued. The woman clearly wasn't letting the matter drop.

"I think I'd remember," Fin said.

"It'll come to me," Mum said, pensive. "I never truly forget a face."

Leaving the tea to brew for a while, I decided it only fair I rescued Fin. There'd been enough excitement that evening already without adding his celebrity status into the mix. I carried my wares over to the table and began passing around cups. "Well," I said to my parents, moving the conversation on. "I didn't expect to be entertaining you two this evening."

"Evidently," Dad said, with a smirk.

Fin suddenly coughed, Dad's humour clearly coming as a surprise.

"Joe," Mum said, nudging my Dad. "Be kind."

"What are you both doing here anyway?" I said, wondering why they had just burst in like that.

Mum scoffed. "We could ask you the same thing."

"Well I asked first," I said, blunt.

"We thought you'd been burgled," Dad replied. "We came to find out what else, if anything, had been taken."

"What are you talking about? Burgled?" Having been in all day, I was sure I'd have noticed.

"Then when we saw the lights on," Mum said. "We thought

whoever it was had obviously come back, so why not catch them in the act."

Dad chuckled. "Oh, we did that, all right."

Mum gave Dad a dirty look, while Fin tried to hide his amusement.

"But what made you think someone had broken in in the first place?" I asked, wanting to get to the bottom of things.

"Because of your car," Mum replied.

I recalled the fact that Fin had borrowed it.

"Some bloke drove passed the house in it this afternoon. And with you being away..."

Fin froze. Like me, he'd obviously realised they were talking about him. I looked at the wall clock, telling myself it was a good job I hadn't, in fact, been burgled. That vehicle had been back for hours and a robber could have been off with the house's entire contents in that time.

"A dodgy-looking fella," Dad continued. He turned his attention to Fin. "I got a good look, on account of him slowing down as he passed."

Fin tried not to smile.

"Dodgy, you say?" I said, smirking Fin's way.

"Definitely. He had blond hair, brushed back off his face," Mum said. "And a solid square jaw." She turned to Fin. "He looked a bit like you."

"Oh, yes," Dad said, clearly still picturing Fin's drive-by. "It seems even criminals appreciate a good set of Christmas lights."

Fin's eyes widened as he made the connection. "So that's your house?" he said, all smiles. "The one with the sleigh on the roof and the giant blow-up Santa?"

My parents nodded.

Fin turned his attention to me. "Why didn't you say?"

"You mean it was you who drove by?" Mum asked. She

leaned back in her seat, her relief evident. "Well that explains things."

"Explains what?" I asked.

"Why I thought I'd seen him before." She indicated Fin. "He's the burglar."

It appeared Mum wasn't the only one feeling relief. "I am he," Fin said, a bit too jovially. Putting a hand up in the air to confirm, he was clearly pleased Mum hadn't recognised him off the telly.

Eyeing his delight, I wondered what his response would have been had my mother given up his real identity, forced to suppose I'd never know. "Mum, he's not a burglar," I said. "He took the car with my permission."

"Fantastic light show, by the way," Fin said to my Dad.

"Please don't encourage them," I said, shaking my head as I went back to collect the teapot.

"You still haven't told us what *you're* doing here?" Mum said.

"The holiday company cancelled my trip," I replied. Not wanting to admit that Jeremy had stung me again, especially in front of Fin, I tried to come up with an excuse. "The resort went down with some stomach bug."

"Really?" Mum said. She straightened up in her seat.

I didn't have to look at her to know her eyes had lit up and steeling myself ready for her onslaught, I began counting backwards. *Three, two, one...*

"Well that is good news," she said, right on cue.

I shook my head. "Tell that to the poor souls who caught it."

Mum nudged my Dad with her elbow, her excitement undeniable. "Joe, you know what this means, don't you? Holly can come home for Christmas."

I poured everyone a drink. "Unfortunately," I said, refusing to let Mum get carried away.

Mum's face fell, her eyes narrowing as she waited to hear what I had to say.

"I've made other arrangements."

Fin swooped in for his cup, no doubt, to hide behind should a family argument ensue.

Dad chuckled. "We can see that," he said, grinning at Fin, while mid-sip, Fin nearly choked on his tea.

"What are you talking about?" Mum asked. "What other arrangements?"

"I've decided to have a staycation."

"A what?" Mum asked.

Fin leaned forward. "It's when instead of..."

I watched Mum flash him a look, silencing his explanation. It was the exact same expression Vee had used when Fin had tried to enlighten her on the matter. "I'll get the biscuits, shall I?" he said, getting up from his seat to fetch some.

"Rubbish!" Mum said, refusing to hear a word of it. "If you're not going on holiday of course you're coming to us for Christmas."

Fin returned with a plate of digestives and placed them in the middle of the table. Re-taking his seat, he picked up his tea again and began drinking.

Mum smiled. "And your boyfriend can come too."

Fin nearly choked for a second time.

I closed my eyes for a second, wishing Mum hadn't just said that. Especially when I couldn't deny the relationship status she'd just bestowed, not after the way my parents had just walked in on us.

"Mum," I said. With no choice but to move the conversation on, I was determined to at least clarify that I would not be changing my plans for Christmas Day yet again.

"Which reminds me," she said to Fin, interrupting my protest before it began. "We haven't been properly introduced."

Dad picked up the mantle. "This is Maz," he said, indicating Mum.

"Excuse me," Mum said. "Sunday names, please. We don't want this young man thinking we're riff-raff.

Please don't, I silently pleaded.

"Sorry, love," he said, starting again. "This is Mary." He indicated my mother.

I cringed, knowing after what was about to follow, Fin would never let me live it down.

"And I'm Joseph." Dad held his hand out.

Fin's eyes widened as he accepted Dad's gesture. He looked my way as if asking if my parents were for real, before returning his attention to them. "Pleased to meet you..." He paused.

I could see he was doing his utmost not to laugh.

"Mary and Joseph."

"And you are?" Dad asked.

"Oh, sorry yes," he said, needing to take control of his voice. "I'm Fin. It's short for Finlay."

"Now you've just got Holly's sister to meet," Mum said.

Oh, Lordy, I thought.

"You'll like Ivy."

"Excuse me?" Fin asked. He put his elbow on the table and rested his hand against his mouth to hide his sniggering.

"Holly's sister," Mum said. "Ivy."

Fin turned to look at me again, biting down on his finger clearly to stop himself from laughing out loud.

Not that his reaction surprised me. My sister and I had been putting up with the same kind of response since we were children. Fin obviously hadn't realised what Vee was short for, and as I looked from Fin, who was desperately trying not to lose control, to Mum and Dad, in their matching Santa outfits, I wanted to hang my head in shame for having what had to be the most embarrassing family on the planet.

"Hang on a minute," Mum said, as if her mind was suddenly somewhere else. "Fin. Fin. Finlay. Finlay Mc..." She slowly turned to look at him, her excitement growing in front of everyone's eyes. "Oh. My. Word," she said. "It's you."

Fin's sniggering stopped.

26

"I can't believe it, Joe," Mum said as she and Dad headed down the hall to the front door. "Not only are we back to having the whole family over for Christmas Day like we always do, we'll have an eminent TV chef dining with us too." She giggled, clearly excited at having finally got what she'd wanted and more.

I rolled my eyes as Fin and I followed behind. "Neither of us actually agreed to that, Mum," I said.

She turned to look at us, stopping Fin and me in our tracks, and ignoring my words, squealed in delight. "You've both made me so happy."

Dad turned too. His expression full of mock desperation, as if knowing he was never going to hear the end of it.

Mum chattered, revelling in her good fortune as she and Dad headed for their car, got in and drove away, while Fin and I stood in silence waving them off. My parents' vehicle disappeared, and, at last, we closed the door on the outside world.

As we retraced our steps back to the kitchen, I couldn't believe the week I was having. On the one hand, I'd been caught up in a high-speed whirlwind, on the other I seemed to have experienced the longest six days of my life, so much had happened.

First I was going on the holiday of a lifetime, then I wasn't. I had a temporary house guest, who turned into a longer-term house guest... and the hottest star in TV cookery. A TV star who I'd been about to have sex with. I'd planned a staycation that involved locking myself away from civilisation for ten whole days of blissful solitude, which had suddenly gone from *me time* to *don't knock, just let yourself in* time. And to top it off, I had a heavily pregnant hormonal sister who had developed paranoid tendencies regarding our mother. *Merry bloody Christmas*, I thought to myself.

"I need a drink," I said, as we entered the room.

"I think I'll join you," Fin replied.

While he took a bottle of wine out of the fridge, I got a couple of glasses from the cupboard. Drinks poured, we sat at the table in silence, as if neither of us knew quite what to say.

Fin appeared pensive, his usual confidence seemingly gone. I waited for him to broach the subject of his stardom. After all, his quiet on the matter was rather pointless considering Mum had outed him for his celebrity status.

"I'm sorry," he eventually said. "I should have told you."

"Why didn't you?" I asked, twiddling my wine glass back and forth between my hands. I might have already known Fin's secret, but I was still interested to know why he had kept it to himself.

He drank a mouthful of wine. "Lots of reasons. You probably wouldn't understand."

"Try me," I said, before putting my glass to my mouth.

He took a deep breath as if gathering his thoughts. "To start with, you saw Roberta."

I scowled. *Boy, did I.* That woman didn't seem to know the meaning of the word *discretion*. All that fluttering of her eyelashes, the sickly-sweet voice, both from the second she met Fin. The woman clearly had no shame. As for her sugar request... My eyes were automatically drawn to the offending cupboard, knowing there weren't many people around who'd had the pleasure of being stuffed into such a small space, forced to listen in on other people's conversations. Yet one more thing to add to my list of that week's reasons to be cheerful.

"And then there was your Mum just then."

I frowned, wondering what he meant by that. I felt defensive on Mum's behalf. I, of all people, knew my mother could be an oddball and it had been pretty evident to everyone concerned that she'd struggled to suppress her enthusiasm at meeting Fin. However, she was hardly in the same category as my self-serving neighbour. "Mum is nothing like Roberta," I said. "Just because she asked you for your autograph and to have her photo taken with you..."

"That's not what I meant."

"Oh. Then what did you mean?"

"That it's just nice to be me sometimes. Without having to smile for the camera."

"Well as long as we've got that straight."

"People have a distorted impression of who I am and that's the version everyone wants to meet. I don't blame them, of course. Why would anyone expect me to be any different from the man zooming into their living room every week. I'm just not sure how to handle all the attention. To find that balance of giving people what they want, while being true to myself. If I'm honest, I find it a bit terrifying. People invest in that show."

I considered my day's viewing, unable to deny the man had a point on that score.

"And the last thing I want is to let anyone down." He paused to take another drink. "I'm not sure I'm explaining myself very well."

"No, I get it. Sort of." Although I wasn't sure if I should feel sorry for the man or shake him. There were people with far worse problems to contend with than fame and fortune.

"And then there's you."

"Okay," I said. The way Fin was talking, I dreaded to think what he was about to say. "What about me?"

"With you, everything is real. Around you I *can* be myself because there are no expectations. Or at least there weren't when you didn't know all this stuff."

"Who says I didn't?"

"Well, did you?" He tilted his head and raised an eyebrow. "You *can* remember what you were wearing when we first met, can't you?"

I let out a laugh. "Oh, so as well as wanting your photo, everyone dresses up for you now, do they?"

Fin chuckled. "I'm not saying that. But they do tend to have brushed their hair."

I recalled standing on the doorstep when Fin first landed, with my scruffy bedhead and the previous night's make-up smeared down my cheeks. "I'll have to give you that one. Maybe I'd have washed my face."

Fin smiled. "Then there was that first morning when I made breakfast."

"That omelette," I said, recalling how good it was. "It really was to die for."

"And that's my point," Fin said, his whole demeanour lighting up. "Watching you enjoy something, not because some chap off the television made it, but because it tasted good. You were the same with the pancakes. You didn't turn your nose up because they came with red noses and antlers. You saw the fun in them. These days everyone seems so serious when it comes to cooking. So pretentious. You remind me of why I became a chef

154

in the first place. To make good simple food that people enjoy eating."

"You don't like what you're doing now?" I asked.

"I like being part of a successful TV show and how it's instilled a joy of cooking in a whole nation. I like getting to know the contestants and seeing the fire in their bellies. That's what drives them to be the best. I love that I'm able to play a part when it comes to their individual journeys, helping them along the way, and hopefully making them better chefs." He scoffed. "And there's no denying the pay's pretty good."

I could only imagine.

"What I don't like is all the extras that come with it. Like the stuff I mentioned before. I know there's good and bad in every job but being out there can be hard sometimes." He indicated to the window and streets beyond, before turning his attention back to me. "I've hosted TV shows in the US, but they were for more niche channels and the audiences weren't as big. In my day-to-day life I could carry on pretty much the same as I always did. Then I came here to do *Cooking Hell*, although at the time none of us knew what we were getting into. No one involved predicted how big it was going to be. It was as if overnight I became public property."

"None of that explains why you didn't tell me about it all though. From what you've said you must have known it would come out at some point?"

"I was trying to hold on to the bit of anonymity you'd given me, I suppose. Plus, I was scared."

"Of what? Not of me, surely?"

"I was scared things would change. That you'd change. Come over all..."

"Fangirl?"

Fin smiled. "I was going to say weird."

"I'm already that."

Fin let out another chuckle. "Seriously, this is your home. The last thing I wanted was for you to feel uncomfortable. Like you had to tread on eggshells, to think about what you were doing or saying all the time. And *I* didn't want to have to do that either. If you'd known, neither of us could be ourselves."

"That's where you're wrong," I said.

Fin furrowed his brow. "What do you mean?"

While he was being honest, I told myself it was time I was truthful too. I got up from my seat and headed over to the sideboard. Opening a drawer, I pulled out Fin's cookbook and returning to the table, placed it down in front of him.

He looked from the book to me. "So you did know?" he asked, clearly confused.

"Not at first. Remember when I said Annie had given me a gift?"

"You mean this was it?"

I nodded. "She'd told me all about you apparently, the night we were drowning our sorrows. Then clicked that I couldn't remember a word of what she'd said. This was her idea of a joke."

"Good old Annie," Fin replied, smiling. "That's just the kind of thing Elliott would have done." He picked up the book and studied the blurb on the back cover, before flipping it over to the front. "I've always hated that photo," he said.

"By then it was pretty obvious you weren't going to mention your illustrious career. So, I hid that away and left things as they were."

"I see."

"No, Fin. I don't think you do. If you did, you'd know that not everyone wants a piece of you. There are people out there happy to let you do what you do *and* be yourself. People like me."

Fin smiled, looking at me with the same degree of intensity

I'd seen before. "So why did *you* keep quiet?" he asked. "Most people would have blurted it out as soon as they realised."

I giggled. "Like Mum, you mean."

"I didn't like to say, but yes."

"A few reasons," I replied. "Like you, I worried the dynamic between us would change. We seemed to be rubbing along nicely and as much as I want to be comfortable in my own home, you're a guest so I want you to be comfortable too. Plus, if I'm honest, I didn't want you to think I'm in any way like Roberta."

"There's no chance of that."

"Good. Because I couldn't fawn over anyone." I took a sip of my wine, at the same time feeling the need to say something. "You do know how lucky you are though, don't you? Because being on telly is the stuff of dreams for most people. That's why you get the likes of Mum who are excited to meet you, as well as the Robertas who see an opportunity to get the life they've always fantasised about. I'm not saying it's right that people behave a certain way, or that it's easy to deal with a lot of the time. But you can understand it, can't you?"

Fin stared at me again, before a gentle smile appeared on his lips. He got up from his seat, before hauling me onto my feet too. "You're one special lady, do you know that?"

"I do. But thank you for acknowledging it."

"Modest too." Fin pulled me close. "I like that."

I smiled, feeling his arms around my waist. "Enough to get back to where we were before Mum and Dad arrived?

Fin's eyes lit up. "So you do want a piece of me?"

"Oh, yes," I replied.

27

I began to awaken, the beginnings of a smile forming on my lips as I sleepily recalled the lustful night I'd shared with Fin. I'd enjoyed the best sex ever – was there no end to the man's talents? I opened my eyes, my smile turning into a grin as I saw Fin, wide awake, staring back at me.

"Good morning, beautiful," he said.

For once I didn't take Fin's compliment as teasing. The previous night he'd proven he found me as attractive as I found him. He'd caressed, kissed, and taken pleasure in every flaw, lump and bump on my body. My smile turned naughty just thinking about it. *As had I.* Fin hadn't just said I was beautiful, he'd made me feel it too. "Good morning."

He leaned towards me and gave me a gentle, lingering kiss before speaking again. "Breakfast?" he asked.

I watched him climb out of bed and taking in his naked body, thought of better things to do than eat.

"I think we worked up quite an appetite last night," he said, winking at me before heading out onto the landing. "Don't you?"

I lay there, giggling about the night we'd had, unable to believe the only thing on Fin's mind was food.

I listened to his bare feet padding along the wooden floorboards into the spare room, then back out and into the bathroom. I heard the shower switch on, and I smiled to myself as his voice rang out over the sound of the water running. I'd grown used to his serenades. A different Christmas carol every morning, that day I was treated to a rendition of *O Christmas Tree.*

While Fin continued to sing, I stretched myself out, feeling like the luckiest woman alive. *Who'd have thought it?* I silently asked. *Finlay McCormack and me?* However, growing fed up of my own company, I climbed out of bed. Smiling, I put on my dressing gown and telling myself that Fin, no doubt, was lonely too, I went to join him in the shower.

I wanted to pinch myself as I made my way down to the kitchen. I felt warm and fuzzy and I knew it was thanks to Fin. He made me feel valued, in a way no other man had done before. I paused in the doorway, taking a moment to observe Fin as he added quartered mushrooms and tomatoes to a pan of frying sliced onions. The whole dish smelt delicious and breathing in the aroma, I realised Fin was right. We had worked up an appetite. I wondered what he was thinking as he cooked. He wore a seriousness on his face. Then again he was an expert at work.

"There you are," Fin said. At last clocking my presence, he replaced his earnestness with a smile. "Coffee?"

"Anything I can do to help?" I asked.

"Nope. Everything's in hand."

I took a seat at the table and while Fin turned his attention to poaching a couple of eggs, I couldn't help but observe how at home he looked. I sighed. Fin wasn't just a great cook, everything about the man seemed perfect and feeling a sense of contentment, I quite happily saw him as a permanent fixture. I was glad my Christmas plans hadn't worked out. Fin's presence beat sunning myself in the Caribbean and a home-alone staycation hands down and I imagined us in a proper relationship, doing all the things proper couples do.

A pang in my chest reminded me that no matter how many flights of fancy I had, Fin would be moving on soon. Not that I blamed the man. With a career like his, he, no doubt, had bigger and better places to be.

"You okay?" he asked. He placed my breakfast in front of me.

"Yes," I replied, keeping my voice light. "Just thinking."

He leaned down, kissed the top of my head and without saying another word sat down to eat too. He seemed preoccupied in his own thoughts again and I felt dread. He probably knew that I'd let my mind run away with me and couldn't bring himself to tell me I was being daft; we had no future.

I picked my fork up and distracted myself by pushing my food around my plate. As wonderful as the meal looked, I was no longer in the mood for it. I snuck a peek at Fin, who sat observing me in return. He reached out, took my hand and gave it a squeeze. An action that felt more final than reassuring.

The front door sounded and as we both looked towards the hallway, Fin didn't release his hold.

"It's only us," Vee called out. "Are you both decent?"

Fin stifled a laugh while I sat there, mortified. "It's not funny," I said, at the same time relieved the disquiet between us had been broken. I imagined Mum racing home after her visit, desperate to get straight on the phone to Vee, to share not just Fin's identity, but also the fact that she and Dad had caught us half naked. "I should have known my parents wouldn't be able keep things to themselves," I said.

My sister popped her head around the door. "Can we come in?" she asked, as if unsure as to whether she'd be welcome or not.

"Of course you can," I replied. I picked up mine and Fin's breakfast plates and carried them over to the kitchen, while Vee stepped into the room, with my brother-in-law right behind. She appeared sheepish, although I supposed she should, considering her behaviour during her last visit.

Mitch nudged her, gesturing for her to keep moving.

"All right, all right," Vee said, keeping her voice low, clearly in the hope that me and Fin wouldn't hear. As she did as she was told, she took a deep breath, as if preparing to speak. "I came to apologise," she said. Unable to make eye contact with either Fin or me, she looked up at the ceiling. "For the way I spoke to you the other day." She looked to her husband as if asking if he was happy with that, but his expression suggested she hadn't quite finished. Vee rolled her eyes like a resentful teenager, before turning to her audience once more. "I had no right to behave the way I did."

"No, you didn't," I replied, trying not to laugh at her performance. "But seeing as you're pregnant, I'll let you off." I turned my attention to Fin. "What about you, Fin? Does my sister have your forgiveness?"

He pretended to think for a moment. "I'd say so," he replied.

I could see he was trying not to laugh too.

"Thank goodness that's over with," Vee said, taking a seat at the table.

Mitch rolled his eyes and shook his head as if resigning himself to the fact that as far as an apology from his wife went, that was the best we were going to get. "Mind if I make a coffee?" he asked, heading for the machine. "Anyone else want one?"

"We're fine thanks," I replied, indicating mine and Fin's cups. "But help yourself."

Vee reached into her bag and I cringed as she pulled out Fin's cookbook. "You wouldn't mind, would you?" she asked, also producing a pen.

I glared at her, wondering how she could be so shameless. "Subtle, Vee. Subtle."

"What?" she said, pushing the book towards Fin.

Fin smiled, while I wanted to die. "It's okay. I don't mind," he said.

I scowled at Vee, while Fin opened the cover and signed his name.

"Thank you," my sister said. She giggled as she took the book back, before opening it up to look at his signature and hugging it to her chest.

Fin's phone began to ring. "Sorry," he said, clearly embarrassed by the interruption. Pulling his mobile out of his pocket he checked the number. "You don't mind if I get this, do you?" He nodded to the garden where he could take the call in private.

"Not at all," I replied. "You go ahead."

He smiled as he headed out, but as I watched him make his exit, as soon as he started speaking his expression changed and he came over all serious. As he paced up and down, Fin caught me looking at him and immediately turned his back on me.

28

"Well you kept quiet," Vee said, bringing my attention back into the room. "Why didn't you tell me your new boyfriend's bloody famous?"

I tilted my head as I looked at her. "Firstly, how could you just embarrass me like that? And secondly, he's not my boyfriend."

"That's not what we heard," Mitch said, chuckling.

It was one thing my brother-in-law knowing about my sex life, but way too yucky for him to discuss it. I flashed him a look, warning him not to go there.

"Sorry," he said. "I couldn't resist."

Vee looked at me, confused. "If he's not your boyfriend, then what is he?"

I stared out into the garden again. Still on the phone, Fin paced up and down. I smiled as I watched him. Taking a deep breath, I sighed. As much as I wanted Fin to stay I knew that wasn't an option. "A Christmas holiday romance," I said.

"Well whatever's going on between you, one thing's for sure. I wouldn't have come in here shouting my mouth off the way I had if I'd realised who he is," Vee replied.

"You save your rudeness for us mere mortals, do you?"

Mitch chuckled from over in the kitchen.

Vee frowned. "You know what I mean."

I smirked as I recalled her strop. "So, if you had been aware, you wouldn't have accused him of being the reason I haven't gone on holiday?"

Vee squirmed. "Please don't."

"Or cut him dead when he tried to explain what a staycation is?"

"I mean it, Holly. I feel embarrassed enough. For you as much as for myself. The man must think we're all mad."

I scoffed. "And he'd be blooming right," I replied. "We are all mad."

"I can vouch for that," Mitch said.

"So where did you meet him?" Vee asked. "It's not like you ever go anywhere except work and the local pub."

I picked up my coffee and took a drink. "He just turned up on my doorstep one morning wanting a bed for the night," I replied, matter of fact.

Vee looked at me suspiciously. "You are joking, right?"

"Nope. I haven't been able to get rid of the man since."

"And now for the real story?" my sister said, refusing to believe a word of it.

I put my cup back down with a smile. "Honestly, it's true. Although he is a relative of Annie's husband. Fin was meant to be staying at Annie's but when Emma landed back home having left her boyfriend, I was asked to put him up instead."

"Emma left Josh?" Vee looked at me confused.

"Yes, but that was days ago, they're back together now. Except there's still no spare bed available for Fin, as both Emma *and* Josh are now staying at Annie's on account of Emma being pregnant." That sounded confusing even to me.

"Emma's pregnant?" Vee's eyes widened.

"She certainly is."

"I can't believe I didn't know any of this." Vee turned to her husband, her shock continuing. "Did you know?" My sister clearly took after our Mum when it came to keeping up with everyone's lives.

"We have had more important things to think about," he replied, indicating his wife's belly.

I fell serious, acknowledging that they had indeed. I recalled her fear that Mum would do anything to get a Christmas baby. "About what you said? Regarding Mum..."

Vee's shoulders slumped. "To be honest, Holly, I don't know where my head's been at lately. I just overreacted over her calling the baby JC."

Jesus Christ. I still couldn't get over that.

"I haven't a clue what's wrong with me. I seem to be losing the plot a lot lately."

"It's her hormones," Mitch said. "But will she listen."

Vee looked his way, her expression stern.

"I'm just saying," her husband replied. "It's nothing to worry about, it's all part of the pregnancy journey."

Vee shook her head. "If I've told him to shut up about what's going on in *my* body once, I've told him a hundred times." She took a deep breath, appearing to try and calm herself. "Anyway," Vee said. "I believe the *good news* is that you're coming to Mum and Dad's on Christmas Day. And I believe Fin will also be in attendance."

"About that," I said. "I still haven't properly talked to Fin about it, let alone decided on–"

"You have to come," Vee said interrupting me.

I knew an act when I saw one.

"I need you there to help me and Mitch protect this one." She rubbed her belly.

I laughed. "Please don't start that again."

My sister smiled. "I will if it means you'll agree to come," she said. "Why should we be the only ones to suffer? Besides you can't say no. Mum and Dad are expecting you both. Plus Mum's checking and re-checking the menu especially for Fin."

Fin suddenly appeared, having let himself back in from the garden. "What's being re-checked especially for me?" he asked.

He might have been smiling as he tucked his phone into his pocket but – unusual for him – his smile didn't quite reach his eyes. It seemed all wasn't as well as Fin evidently tried to portray.

"Everything okay?" I asked.

He nodded, fast turning back to my sister and brother-in-law.

"The Christmas Day menu has a few additions this year," Mitch replied. "You're being honoured, mate."

"I've told them we haven't actually agreed to go yet," I said, partly because I didn't want Fin to feel bullied and partly because I still wasn't sure if I wanted to attend.

"But why wouldn't we?" he asked, instead.

My heart sank. I had hoped Fin would want to celebrate here at my house, just the two of us. I wanted to kick myself for letting my mind get carried away with itself that morning. I'd obviously freaked the man out. Fin, having realised what I was thinking, was plainly trying to distance himself.

"I'm happy to if you are?" Fin said to me. "I can't think of anything better than a proper family Christmas."

I reminded myself about what Annie had said regarding Fin's parents. Aloof, she'd called them. I supposed Fin's Christmases would have been polite affairs, nothing like the in-your-face celebrations I'd grown up with. If Fin's parents had been distant, it was no wonder Fin preferred a livelier environment in which to celebrate. "Mum and Dad's it is," I said.

"Brilliant," Vee said with a satisfied smile. "That's settled."

"You don't know what you're letting yourself in for," Mitch said to Fin.

Knowing my family, I could think of a myriad of things.

Fin gave me a fleeting glance, that I was sure I wasn't meant to see. "I can't wait to find out," he replied.

With everyone else looking so happy, I tried to raise a smile. It seemed my Christmas holiday romance was coming to an end.

29

With Vee and Mitch gone, there was no hiding from the tension between Fin and me. Needing a distraction, I set about washing up the breakfast dishes.

Fin approached with a tea towel to dry them, his smile pinched as he picked up a plate and got on with it.

The atmosphere between us had changed. The fun and passion we'd experienced on waking up had been replaced by an edginess, as if both of us were aware of the inevitable but didn't know how to behave because of it. I told myself that instead of being naïve and throwing caution to the wind, I should have realised if we jumped into bed together relations would become strained. I'd never been one for one-night stands or friends with benefits, so it stood to reason I'd end up wanting something Fin was in no position to give.

"Are you sure about going to Mum and Dad's?" I asked. It would have been easy to stay quiet. To take Fin on his word and pretend he wasn't going anywhere any time soon. However, pushing my unease to one side, it felt only right I provided Fin with a way out. "There's still time to change your mind."

My question appeared to surprise Fin. "Don't you want me there?" he asked.

Staring into the washing-up bowl, I wanted nothing more. "It's not that," I replied, unable to look at him. "Vee did put you on the spot a bit and then there's last night to consider." I made sure to keep my tone light. "I wouldn't want you agreeing to something because you felt you had to."

He put the tea towel down and taking my wet hands, pulled me round to face him. His expression showed concern, as if what I thought mattered. "Do you honestly think I'm the type of guy to sleep with a woman and run?" he asked.

I hoped not.

"Last night was special." He searched my face. "Wasn't it?"

I nodded.

"So, if you want to spend Christmas Day at your parents' house, then I do too."

Looking back at Fin, he appeared genuine, but I couldn't shift the nagging doubt that all wasn't as it should be. There had to be something the man wasn't telling me. "Okay," I replied.

"Besides, my first family Christmas in years, in a house that's got so many lights I bet I could see it from space. Who'd say no to an opportunity like that?"

I chuckled. Most people thought my parents barmy for going all out the way they did, yet there was Fin positively loving it. I thought back to the previous Christmas when I'd had to put up with Jeremy's not-so-well-disguised reluctance. I smiled. "Only if you're sure?"

Fin looked confused. "Why wouldn't I be?"

I turned back to the washing up. "No reason."

Fin pulled me round to face him for a second time. "Holly? What's going on?"

My face crumpled. "You seem different," I said. "*We* seem

different. It's as if you have something on your mind, but you can't bring yourself to say it."

Fin put a hand up to rub his forehead. "Okay. If you must know, there is something."

I felt dread as he took my hand and led me over to the table. Sitting down, I steeled myself ready to experience the ultimate in embarrassment – getting dumped from a relationship that wasn't even a relationship.

"That call just now," Fin said, taking the seat next to me.

I stared down at my knees wondering if I was about to learn he had a wife and three kids after all.

"It was about work."

I lifted my gaze to look at him, confused as to what that had to do with me and his change in attitude.

"I've been asked to front a new project. I had an idea the call was coming, it's why I had to go to Leeds the other day."

"Okay," I said, my bewilderment continuing. "But that's a good thing, isn't it?"

Fin smiled. "I suppose it is, yes."

"Another exciting project like *Cooking Hell*?"

"Not quite the same, but exciting nonetheless."

I waited for him to expand, but he stayed quiet. "Well?" I asked, eager to know more.

"Well nothing."

I rose to my feet, ready to get on with the washing up, at the same time insisting I didn't care anyway. "You don't have to tell me if you don't want to," I said. "It's not as if it's any of my business."

Fin took my hand, preventing me from moving. "It's in America. The project. That's where they're sending me."

I plonked myself back down in my seat. "Oh." I looked down at my knees again, unable to meet Fin's gaze once more.

"I've been asked to host one of those travel-come-cookery

shows. You know the kind, going from town to town, sampling local cuisine and at the end of each episode replicating what's been eaten for the viewers at home."

"Sounds fun," I said. Pleased for him but not so much for me, I tried to sound upbeat. The last thing I wanted was to come across like some needy girlfriend, even though I was neither. I pulled at my fingernails. "When do you leave?"

"On the 31st."

I lifted my head to look at Fin, feeling relieved. "Of January? But that's weeks away yet."

"Of December," Fin replied.

"I see." I took heart in the disappointment on his face, which matched my feelings. "But that's only a week or so away. It's New Year's Eve," I said, my voice quiet.

Fin got up from his seat, hauled me up out of mine, and pulled me into a bear hug. "Looks like we're going to have to make the most of this family Christmas of yours, doesn't it?" he said, kissing my forehead.

With his arms wrapped tight around me, I breathed in his scent, wanting that moment to last forever.

Fin leaned back to look at me. "Can we do that?"

I nodded, unable to find any words.

30

CHRISTMAS EVE

Having woken up far too early, I lay in the darkness staring up to the ceiling and listening to the rhythm of Fin's gentle breathing. Light from a street lamp shone through a gap in the curtain and I turned onto my side to look at the man lying next to me. He slept on his back, one hand behind his head. The bedcovers were down to his waist, enabling me to watch the rise and fall of his chest as he inhaled and exhaled. Knowing our Christmas holiday romance would soon be at an end, I'd already started to miss him. "I think I've fallen in love with you, Fin McCormack," I whispered. I hardly believed it possible, considering I'd only met him a week ago.

Fin began shifting position and as he slowly turned my way I froze. My heart skipped a beat at the thought of him opening his eyes having heard me. I held my breath for a moment, only relaxing once I saw that he hadn't actually awakened. There was no way Fin could know how I felt about him and as he stayed asleep, it seemed my secret was still mine to keep.

With Fin stirring, I knew it wouldn't be long before he woke up for real and I slid out of bed, before heading downstairs to put some coffee on in readiness. Waiting for the machine to work its magic, I became aware of how quiet and lonely the house was going to be without Fin. Especially the kitchen, which had understandably, yet inadvertently, turned into his domain. I smiled as I imagined him flitting between the cooker, the fridge, and the sink, producing fabulous meal after fabulous meal for us both. Some with names I couldn't pronounce let alone try to recreate.

Contemplating how much cooking Fin had done since landing, I thought what better morning to return the gesture than Christmas Eve morning. While my culinary skills might not have stretched to the fancy food Fin served up, as I plugged in the toaster and dug out the frying pan, I knew I made a mean bacon sandwich.

With the bacon sizzling to perfection, crispy on the edges but not burnt in the middle, the kitchen smelt divine. Turning the heat off I grabbed a couple of golden slices of toast, slathered them in real butter and with a bottle of brown sauce at the ready, began the sandwich's construction.

Hearing Fin make his way downstairs, I quickly finished what I was doing and poured him a cup of coffee.

Waiting for him to enter, I frowned at the sound of his voice, realising he must have been chatting on his phone. I couldn't hear his conversation as he spoke in hushed tones, although I assumed the call was work-related seeing as he was speaking so quietly. We'd made an agreement that we wouldn't talk about his new job. The plan was to forget about it for as long as was feasible and simply enjoy the time we had left together. Pushing all thoughts of his leaving to the back of my mind, it was a plan I was determined to see through.

"Thank you. Anyway, I've got to go. Bye," Fin said just before he entered the room. Then he addressed me, plastering a smile on his face. "Something smells wonderful." It was good to know he seemed resolute in our strategy too.

I picked up his breakfast and cup of coffee and carried them over to the table. "Merry Christmas," I said, giving him a peck on the lips.

Taking a seat, he smiled at the offering. "A bacon sandwich. The way to a man's heart."

"Pleased to hear it," I said.

As I headed back to pour myself a drink and tidy up the mess I'd made, my mobile beeped, signalling I had a text come through. I picked the phone up off the kitchen counter, surprised to see Annie's name on the screen. Having assumed she would be far too busy on Christmas Eve to be contacting anyone let alone me, I opened her message, curious as I read.

You free for coffee today? I finish work at one.

I grimaced, not sure I fancied tackling a hoard of last-minute shoppers.

"That looks interesting," Fin said, obviously acknowledging my reluctant expression.

"It's from Annie. She wants to meet up later." I put my phone back down.

"Sounds like fun."

I looked Fin's way. "You think? Today of all days, town will be packed."

"She probably needs to let off steam," he said. "What with Emma and her boyfriend taking over the house."

He had a point, I supposed, but I still wasn't sure I was up for it.

"You should go," Fin said, eating his sandwich. "Just because I prefer to lie low, that doesn't mean you have to."

"What if I said I don't want to go?" I walked towards him. "What if I'd prefer to stay here and keep you company?"

Fin laughed as I positioned myself behind him and put my

arms around his chest. I snuggled my face into his neck and gently kissed it.

"I'd say you've been cooped up here with me for long enough. And that whatever you have in mind for entertainment, I'll be ready and waiting when you get back."

"Spoilsport." I released my hold. "Anyone would think you're trying to get rid of me."

"A man does need his rest, you know."

I laughed. We had kept ourselves rather active. "You're probably right, I should go." After all, meeting up with Annie for coffee was the least I could do. If it weren't for her, I wouldn't be enjoying the best Christmas of my life. "A friend in need and all that."

"That's my girl," Fin said.

My heart flipped. *My girl.* Liking the sound of that, I sighed. *If only.*

31

Forced to navigate the crowds, I was breathless by the time I got to the café and then as I entered I was hit with a long queue at the counter. I glanced around and spotted Annie waving at me from a table in the far corner. She pointed to a drink already waiting for me but I knew thanks to the time that that one no doubt was cold and I decided to get us both a fresh cup. I stuck my thumb up acknowledging I'd seen her before joining the line.

Hastening over, I placed our drinks on the table before giving Annie a hug and taking a seat. "Sorry I'm late. Finding a parking space was a nightmare." I looked around at all the diners. "I expected it to be busy, but this has to set a record." To say the place was packed was an understatement.

"Ridiculous, isn't it? I haven't stopped still all morning. It's been frantic over at the bookshop. Thank goodness that's me done for a few days." She looked around, lowering her voice. "Considering it's Christmas Eve, you'd expect most people to be a bit more organised." She picked up her cup and drank a mouthful of coffee. "Although I don't know why I'm so shocked at the number of people out and about. It's the same every year."

"I must say I was surprised when you messaged. I thought you'd be racing home to get sorted for tomorrow? Shouldn't you be stuffing a turkey or peeling veg this afternoon?"

Annie smiled. "No need. It turns out I *won't* be doing all the Christmas Day shenanigans as usual. I'll be putting my feet up like I'd hoped."

I laughed. "So who's going to be running around after you?" I couldn't imagine it being her daughter.

"Josh. He's going to make dinner and is, no doubt, knee deep in vegetable prep as we speak. Apparently, all I need to do is relax."

I was pleased for Annie. It was nice to know that, for once, someone was looking after her. "So how's Emma coping with her pregnancy?" I asked.

Annie frowned. "As well as I'm sure you're imagining."

I chuckled, neither confirming nor denying my thoughts.

"Needless to say, she's taking morning sickness to a whole new level. According to her the experts have got it wrong, it's twenty-four seven sickness. Not that the girl's nausea has stopped her eating for two, I might add." She took another drink. "Poor Josh is picking up after her nearly every minute of the day. Fetching and carrying for her like there's no tomorrow. Because we all know being pregnant prevents a woman from using her legs. The lad must be exhausted." Annie rolled her eyes, while I giggled imagining the scene. "Other than that, she seems to be handling it pretty well."

"And what about you? How are you managing?"

"Oh, I'm okay. Still getting used to having a full house. Although on a positive note I'm loving the fact that I'm going to be a grandmother." She sighed. "I'm just hoping I'll do a better job of being a grandparent, because I wouldn't win any awards as a mum."

I frowned, her words saddening me. "Don't say that, Annie. You're a great mum."

Annie's expression froze as she looked at me. "You have met my daughter, haven't you?"

"You shouldn't be so hard on yourself," I said. "Being a single parent isn't easy."

Her face relaxed again as she took a deep breath and inhaled. "I know. I just sometimes think if Elliott had lived, Emma might have turned out differently. Less demanding, maybe? I think when her dad died, I overcompensated. Spoiled her, to try and make up for her grief. She was dealing with so much and at such a young age. I suppose I gave her what she wanted when she wanted it to try and ease things a little." Annie shook her head. "It's no wonder she thinks the world revolves around her. Thanks to me, that's what she was taught."

"You're beating yourself up unnecessarily. You did what I assume any mother would do. Protect their child from pain."

"And you're just being kind."

"Besides, she'll think otherwise when the baby comes. Once that tiny little bundle lands in her arms, she'll look down and realise he or she is relying on her as much as she's relied on you. That's bound to even the balance."

Annie scoffed. "She's going to have some sort of wake-up call, that's for sure."

"With you there to help her through it."

"I know." She smiled. "And thank you. For listening. Again."

"What are friends for?"

"Anyway, enough about Emma," Annie said. "Let's talk about something cheerier. How are you and Fin getting on?" Annie suddenly developed a twinkle in her eye. "He tells me you're getting along nicely."

I felt myself blush. "Does he now?"

Annie's face froze for a second time. She narrowed her eyes, suspicious, before a grin spread across her face. "O. M. G." It clearly had dawned on her that there was more to Fin and me than she'd initially realised. "You're not saying? You are, aren't you?"

"I'm not saying anything."

Annie squealed in delight, which customers took as an invitation to turn and look at us, all of them clearly wondering why the excitement.

"Keep your voice down," I said, my embarrassment growing. Not that Annie seemed to hear a word I said. I smiled apologetically at the growing number of interested parties, my eyes finally resting on Roberta. *Shit!* I thought as she turned away in apparent disgust. *That's all I need.*

Roberta uttered something to her dining party, who looked my way. Whatever she'd said they appeared equally appalled, before chunnering amongst themselves.

"I want to know everything," Annie said, failing to notice any of the attention we'd garnered. "And don't leave anything out."

I raised an eyebrow, sure she didn't want *all* the details.

"Well, maybe not *everything* everything." She clapped her hands together, her glee showing no sign of abating. "You know, I had an idea you two would be perfect for each other."

I was sure she hadn't.

"Not that I thought anything would actually happen. But I did say he *liked* you, didn't I? This is so thrilling." She paused to look at me direct, her face all at once serious. "Tell me, do I need to buy a hat?"

"No, you don't," I replied. Almost choking on my coffee, I couldn't believe she thought that a possibility.

"Because I'll be wearing a bridesmaid dress?" she asked.

I looked at her, mortified.

"Maid or matron of honour then?" She giggled. "Come on,

Holly, you've got to give me something. You know how much I love a good wedding."

"You need to stop," I said. If I thought I'd let my mind run away with itself, Annie's was leaps and bounds ahead. "We're just enjoying each other's company."

"I'll bet."

"While he's still here," I replied. Disregarding her witticism, I needed her to know that wedding bells were in no way, shape, or form, a part of mine and Fin's future.

"What do you mean?" At last, she fell calm. "He's not going anywhere, is he? At least not for a while?"

"He's been offered another TV project."

Annie's eyes lit up. "Really? That's fantastic!"

"In America."

"Oh." Her shoulders slumped. "Not so fantastic then."

"I'm afraid not. He leaves on the 31st."

"Of January?" Annie asked, in the same way I'd done.

Much to Annie's horror, I shook my head. "December."

Her face fell even further.

32

———

It was late afternoon and already going dark by the time Annie and I wished each other a merry Christmas and bade farewell. We promised to meet up before the New Year, not least because the romantic in Annie wanted to see the "two love birds" together before "fate tore us apart". I shook my head as I recalled her melodrama. When it came to matters of the heart, Annie couldn't seem to help herself.

As I drove out of town, shoppers still milled around, although they were less in number. Most of them, I assumed, had wanted to get home to start their celebrations. My phone began to ring and, rather than pull over to answer, I decided to ignore it. I wanted to get home and out of the cold; if the call was important, whoever it was would leave a message or try again later.

After a few fun hours, laughing, joking and commiserating with Annie, I found myself wondering what Fin had been up to. I couldn't help but think he seemed keen to see me off earlier. Then again, I supposed we had been in each other's pockets those last few days. He probably needed the time to sort out his upcoming travel arrangements and work commitments. Which, considering our agreement not to talk about his departure, he couldn't do with me hanging around the place. With the 31st fast approaching he had to organise himself sooner rather than later.

While I didn't want Fin to leave, no way could I have asked him to stay. Like I'd said, he had a life that the rest of us only dreamed about. There he was, sharing his love of food, brightening up everyone's TV screens, and travelling the world along the way. I couldn't expect him to give that up, especially to live in the quaint yet staid Yorkshire Dales. I scoffed. Fin probably couldn't imagine anything more boring. And even if he wanted to give things a go, I knew he'd only end up resenting me for it.

A part of me envied Fin's achievements. Not that I had any right to. Whereas he'd given his career the level of dedication it needed to succeed, all I'd done since leaving university was plod along in a bookshop. Of course, I enjoyed my job, but it could never be described as high flying. Nor was it living out my childhood dream. My crap existence was one of the reasons why my holiday had felt so important. It would have taken me out of my comfort zone and given me the shake-up I needed. Then again, as I thought about what had happened over the last eight days, wasn't that what Fin had done?

As I pulled up at home, I told myself not to be so miserable. Christmas Eve was no time to be thinking about regrets or what ifs. Grabbing my bag and climbing out of the car, I reminded myself it was a time of fun and celebration.

Carols played as I entered the house, while whatever Fin was cooking smelt delicious as usual. "Only me," I called out, letting him know I was back.

He appeared in the kitchen doorway at the end of the hall. "Hello, gorgeous," he said.

I smiled, knowing I would miss him and his welcome home greetings after he'd gone.

He stepped forward, before pulling the door to behind him and like the gentleman he'd proved himself to be, he approached to relieve me of my scarf and coat.

My mobile began to ring once more, but as I took it out of my bag and saw the caller was Mum, Fin's eager expression told me she could wait and I put it away again, happy to give the man my full attention.

"Close your eyes," Fin said, his face full of excitement.

I recalled the last time Fin had made such a request. On that occasion he'd surprised me with the most randomly yet beautifully decorated Christmas tree and safe in that knowledge, unlike then, I was more than happy to play along. "Okay," I said, looking forward to seeing what delights were to come.

Fin took my arm and led me to the kitchen, before pushing the door open so we could enter. A few steps in he brought me to a standstill. "Open," he said.

My eyes lit up. "You've done all this for me?" I asked.

My table, covered with a white cloth, had been laid for two. In the middle sat a centrepiece made from a masonry jar half-filled with water and cranberries, and trimmed with green leaves and ferns. Lit candles sat in sconces at either side, while two white plates sat on red chargers, each setting finished off with a pale green napkin that had been gathered and tied with red ribbon. Fin had tucked sprigs of greenery into the ribbon to match the centrepiece. The whole ensemble was simple yet pretty and romantic. "But how?" I said, wondering where everything had come from.

"You can probably guess I made a couple of things, like the centrepiece and makeshift napkin holders. But most of it I borrowed from Annie."

"She was in on this?"

Fin laughed. "How else could I get you out of the way? Josh dropped what I needed round while Annie kept you busy."

SUZIE TULLETT

I tried to work out when they could have possibly arranged everything. Aside of his trip to Leeds, Fin and I had been together twenty-four seven for days. "This morning's phone call," I said, realisation dawning. I playfully tapped his chest. "I thought you wanted rid of me for some reason."

Fin put his arms around my waist and pulled me close. "And *I* thought seeing as we're at your parents' tomorrow, we could enjoy a little Christmas celebration of our own tonight. Just the two of us."

"Sounds perfect to me," I replied, stretching up for a lingering kiss.

"I hope you're hungry," he said.

"I'm famished."

Releasing his hold, Fin headed for the kitchen area. "How does a three-cheese fondue with cable knit breadsticks to start sound? Followed by *filet mignon* with shallot butter, home-made oven fries and cream spinach? And because Christmas wouldn't be Christmas without a bit of tradition, fruit and nut trifle to finish?"

"Absolutely wonderful," I said, my stomach and I both in agreement.

I watched him start to gather some of his ingredients together. "Anything I can do to help?" I asked.

"Yes. You can grab this..." He poured me a glass of wine. "And go and read one of those books of yours."

I grinned, telling myself I could get used to being ordered out of the kitchen. "Are you sure you don't want to stay here forever?" I asked.

Handing me my drink, Fin appeared surprised by my question.

"That was a joke," I said. "Of course I don't expect you to give up your hard-earned career." My mobile began to ring again. "I'm going to have to get that," I said. "It'll be Mum. She's already

184

tried twice. If I keep ignoring her she'll be straight round to check we haven't been murdered in our beds. You don't mind, do you?"

"I don't mind at all," Fin replied. "Go. Relax. Say hello from me."

I retrieved my phone from my bag and taking my wine with me headed through to the lounge. "Hi, Mum," I said, taking a seat on the sofa as I answered her call.

"Holly! Where have you been?"

"Whoah!" Forced to pull the handset away from my ear to stop my eardrum from bursting, Mum sounded way more excited than was good for her.

"Why didn't you tell us?" she asked before I could say anything else.

I frowned, wondering what the woman was talking about. "Tell you what?"

Mum giggled. "You know exactly what."

"No, Mum, I don't."

"I can't believe we had to hear it from someone else. You could have phoned to tell us personally. Or better still, popped round."

"Tell Holly I'm opening a bottle of champagne," Dad called out from somewhere in the background, sounding as equally upbeat.

"Dad said he's opening a bottle of champagne."

I shook my head. Wondering if that was their second bottle as neither of my parents seemed to make any sense. "And he wants me to know this because?" I asked.

"To celebrate, of course. It was Joan who told me. She heard it from Sally's mother-in-law's sister."

I rolled my eyes, wishing she'd explain herself better. "Heard what, Mum?"

"About you and Fin, silly."

"Here you are, Maz," Dad said.

"Cheers!" They both called out, to the sound of clinking glasses.

"What about me and Fin?" I asked. I began to wonder if my parents had taken something; something that had clearly impaired their mental capacities.

"Your engagement, of course."

"My what?" My eyes widened in horror.

"For your upcoming wedding."

"What upcoming wedding?" Mum and Dad really had lost the plot.

"The one you were talking about in the café today."

My jaw dropped at the same time as the penny.

"Dad said you were probably saving the news for tomorrow, but sleeping on Christmas Eve is exciting enough. I had to ring to say congratulations."

"I've gotta go, Mum," I said, stunned.

"But..."

"I'll call you later."

Cutting the call, I sat there letting Mum's words sink in, knowing Sally's mother-in-law's sister must have been in the café that afternoon. Having overheard Annie's overzealous comments about hats and bridesmaids and maids and matrons of honour, the woman had put two and two together and got seven.

I put my glass to my lips and poured the whole of its contents down my throat, hoping it would quell the dread I was experiencing. However, it did nothing of the sort. Rising to my feet, I headed to the kitchen, with no clue as to how to explain to Fin that my parents were under the impression we were soon to be betrothed. I felt myself turn green.

Fin looked my way as I entered, his smile fast fading. "Holly?" he asked, clearly recognising the colour change in my face. "What's happened?"

"I'm not sure how to put this," I said. "But it's Mum and Dad."

Fin dropped his knife on the counter. "What about them?" He hastened towards me.

I swallowed hard. "They think we're getting married."

33

CHRISTMAS DAY

"Merry Christmas," Fin said, whispering in my ear.

I opened my eyes to see him standing there, with a great big smile and a tray. "Breakfast in bed. What have I done to deserve this?" I asked, smiling back. I stretched myself out before pulling myself up into a sitting position.

"I thought you deserved a special treat on Christmas morning."

Fin placed the tray on my lap and kissed the top of my head.

"Yummy," I said, looking down at a couple of slices of toast, a perfectly poached egg, and a mug of strong coffee. A little vase with a sprig of heather sat amongst everything, reminding me of our first breakfast together, the morning after he'd arrived. "Thank you."

Fin opened the curtains and light streamed into the room. "What time do we need to be at your parents?" he asked, sitting down on the bed next to me.

I laughed. "If they had their way we'd be there now." I looked at the clock to see it was 9am. "In fact, I'm surprised they haven't rung to ask where we are." I picked up my coffee and took a drink.

"I'm dreading it to be honest. Goodness knows what we're in for when we get there. They'll never believe us when we tell them they've been misinformed and that we're not getting married. Not when the news came from Sally's mother-in-law's sister."

Fin chuckled, while I recalled Mum and Dad's excitement as they talked on the phone. I couldn't believe they'd popped a bottle of champagne in celebration when they'd heard the alleged news third-hand. My parents should have known it was nonsense if it hadn't come from me. "I am sorry," I said, already picturing them throwing theirs arms around Fin, welcoming him to the family.

"Why? It's not your fault."

The man might have had a point, but his response was still impressive. While I felt mortified at being the centre of local gossip, he didn't seem bothered at all. "How do you do it?" I asked. "Take something like this in your stride?"

"I just think everything has a way of working itself out," Fin replied. "Besides, you have to admit it is pretty hilarious."

My inner voice questioned what he meant by that. Hilarious, as in funny? Or hilarious, as in a man like him, with the whole planet at his feet, marrying a woman like me? "For you maybe," I said. I took a deep breath and exhaled. "I can imagine the fallout when you're gone."

Fin reached out and put a hand up to my cheek. "Hey, I thought we weren't going to think about that yet?"

I took in his soft yet serious expression, wondering if it was telling me he found the prospect of his departure as difficult as I did. "You're right," I said, determined to enjoy the time we did have. So what if the gossipmongers thought I'd been dumped, because the Fins of the world didn't seriously get involved with the Hollys. Fin had been mine for seven glorious days and counting and no amount of outside pity or gloating or whatever approach people took with regards to our situation, could change that. "It's all about the now."

Fin looked at me, an eyebrow raised. "It certainly is," he said. Taking my cup, he silently placed it down next to the breakfast plate, before removing the tray out of the way altogether. He pulled off his T-shirt, revealing his broad chest and taut muscles.

Merry Christmas to me, I thought to myself.

I giggled as Fin unzipped his jeans and took them off, before whipping back the duvet and straddling me. As I laid back against my pillow, my gaze inviting him to come and take me, I ran my hands up and down his thighs making sure to get dangerously close to his penis. My skin tingled and my nether regions stirred as he slowly began unbuttoning my pyjama top, all the while keeping his eyes on mine. Boy, was that man sexy.

"God you're beautiful," he said. He leaned forward and brought his face level with mine, pecking my lips with kiss after kiss.

I ran my fingers through his hair as our kisses became more passionate, before his mouth moved towards my ear, his lips at once tender against my neck. His tongue gently moved downwards towards my breasts and I let out a little moan as it began circling one of my nipples. As he expertly repositioned himself, Fin pulled at the drawstring on my bottoms until the waistband loosened enough to let him in. His hand slid down my tummy and I gasped as his hand slipped between my thighs.

34

Freshly showered and dressed, Fin and I sat at the dining table finishing cups of coffee before setting out to Mum and Dad's house. Imagining my parents' excitement, I dreaded to think what we were walking into. Unlike Fin, who'd said he wasn't fazed at all.

Neither of us said anything, but an air of inevitability seemed to have settled between us. As if the suggestion of a long-term relationship such as marriage had only highlighted the fact that for us time was running out. It hurt to think he was soon leaving and there wasn't really anything either of us could do. Although as I stared into my drink, I tried not to think about that. Feeling Fin's eyes on me, I glanced up to find him staring back at me, pensive, his hands wrapped tight around his mug. "What?" I asked, self-conscious.

"I was just thinking how glad I am to have met you."

I felt myself blush, wondering if he was glad enough to stay. "Ditto," I replied, knowing it would have been wrong of me to ask him.

"No. I'm *really* glad I met you."

I thought about what Annie had said about Fin *liking* liking me and I couldn't deny the strength of feeling I had for him. Then again, I probably wasn't the only woman to have fallen for Fin's charms. Every woman he'd met, no doubt, *liked* liked him. If ever there was a man who seemed to have everything it was Fin. Looks, career, confidence, and personality... When Fin did decide to settle down, I knew whoever he ended up with was going to be one lucky woman. "I bet you say that to all the girls," I replied.

"I have something for you," he said. "A Christmas present."

"Really?" I gave him a mischievous smile. "I thought I'd already had that?"

Fin shook his head and chuckled.

He got up and went to the hall, reappearing seconds later with a gift bag. I felt delighted and mortified at the same time. Had I known he was going to get me something, I'd have made sure I could return the gesture.

It wasn't that the issue of gifts hadn't crossed my mind. Of course I'd considered surprising Fin with a little token. But every time I came up with an idea there seemed to be an unspoken message attached. My choice was either too romantic and personal which implied a deeper commitment than Fin had given; or not romantic at all which suggested what we had shared had been meaningless. Coming up with the perfect gift seemed impossible so in the end I'd decided not to bother, in the hope that he hadn't bothered either.

"*Voilà!*" Fin said, a big grin on his face. Placing the bag in front of me, he took the seat to my right.

I looked from the gift to him.

"Go on then." He indicated I dive straight in.

My heart raced as I wondered what it could be, and my hands shook in anticipation. Reaching in, I pulled out a card and the most beautifully put together present. Neatly wrapped in pale blue tissue paper and tied with a matching ribbon, I thought the presentation alone was perfect. It seemed a shame to spoil it, which was why I decided to open the card first.

Fin put a hand out to stop me. "Save that for last," he said, much to my surprise.

Having been taught it was more polite to do things the other way round, I wondered why that particular order mattered. However, as it seemed important to Fin, I did as he requested and put the card to one side, in favour of opening his gift first. I pulled on one end of the ribbon and untied it, before my gaze turned to Fin who clearly looked forward to my response. I giggled as I unwrapped the tissue paper, my eyes widening and my smile growing as my gift revealed itself. "That's so thoughtful," I said.

"It's to get you started on writing that novel you've talked about."

I ran my fingers across the leather-bound journal, knowing if I wasn't careful, I'd cry. I leaned over and kissed Fin, my heart fit to burst thanks to his considerateness. I just wished I had something to give him in return.

Suddenly remembering I did have something, I jumped out of my seat and headed for the sideboard. Opening the top drawer, I paused for a second, hoping I wasn't about to regret my decision. Pulling out the work Secret Santa I'd been gifted, I fixed a smile on my face before turning to Fin. "For you," I said, heading back to the table and handing it over.

Fin smiled. "Thank you. Although you didn't have to, you know."

"I know." Having never been any good at lying, I willed myself not to blush. "But I wanted to." I sat tense wondering what the hell was underneath all that wrapping paper, as Fin started to pick at the reams and reams of Sellotape that covered it. Not an easy task if Fin's struggle was anything to go by.

"You've certainly done a good job of this," he said, grappling.

Finally, Fin had peeled enough away to start tackling the paper – a repetitive wordplay design using the words *Gangsta Wrapper* over and again. "Interesting choice," Fin said, while I sat there with a tight smile.

Finally, the gift began to show itself, leaving me sat there embarrassed.

"A Rubik's Cube," Fin said. The man was clearly doing his utmost to hide his confusion.

Even as I cringed, I told myself I should feel relieved. At least it hadn't come from Richard. I knew from experience if it had, I could have easily have just handed Fin a grow-your-own boyfriend kit. "I thought it might keep you entertained on your long flight," I said, forced to think on my feet.

Fin leaned over and kissed me. "Thank you," he replied. "It most certainly will."

I jumped to my feet and eager to move our focus away from the Secret Santa, thought it was time we got going. "We should probably be setting off–"

"Not so fast," Fin replied, interrupting me.

"What?" I hoped he wasn't expecting me to give the damn Rubik's cube a go.

"We haven't finished yet."

"We haven't?"

Fin nodded to the card he'd given me.

"Oh my word, I'm so sorry," I said and sitting back down I picked it straight up. I smiled at the sight of my name, beautifully written on the front of the envelope. Fin would have to be a dab hand with a pen as well. I flipped the envelope over and sliding my finger under the seal, tore it open. The card had a picture of a colourful floral wreath against a navy-blue background, with the words *Merry Christmas* written in gold at its centre. I opened it up, expecting to read a seasonal message. Taking in Fin's words, however, I thought my heart might stop.

I looked from the card to Fin and back again.

Come with me, he'd simply written.

35

"Are you sure you're all right driving?" Fin asked. "Because you look a bit dazed."

"What do you expect?" I said, swerving to avoid a parked car. "You've just turned my life upside down."

Fin chuckled.

"It's all right for you. You're used to flying across the world at a moment's notice. I'm not."

"Like I've said, I appreciate it's a big ask. And you don't have to give me an answer right now." He put a hand on my leg. "Of course, you need to think everything through. But what can I say, Holly Noelle? I've fallen in love with you."

Every time Fin said those words my heart sang. After all, I'd fallen for him too. But giving up the only life I'd ever known was scary and I wasn't sure I could do it. If I'd had more time to get used to the idea, to plan, and to get my head around what Fin was asking of me, then maybe the decision to fly off into the sunset with him would feel more of an option. But my sister was about to give birth and my parents weren't getting any younger. As for Mum, the prospect of my ten-day holiday had been suffi-cient to send her into a spin, so goodness knew how she was going to react to any suggestion of me leaving for months or even for good. I sighed, as if the thought of having to tell my whole family that Fin and I weren't getting married wasn't bad enough.

"Whatever you decide," Fin said. "We'll make it work."

If he was talking about a long-distance relationship, I wasn't sure we could. Fin had already mentioned seeing other chefs' relationships break down on account of them not being able to spend much time with their partners. America is a long way from the Yorkshire Dales, so the two of us would have even less time together. I put my hand on his and as we continued our journey, I couldn't help but think we were in an all-or-nothing situation.

Vee's car was already outside Mum and Dad's when Fin and I pulled up. "I hope you're ready for this," I said as I took off my seat belt. I felt sick. I knew I said I wanted some excitement in my life, but now I'd overdosed on the stuff.

"Isn't it fantastic?" Fin said, taking in all the lights and decorations adorning my parents' house. "Your mum and dad certainly know how to do Christmas."

"I think you mean they're barking mad."

As if proving my point, before we'd even got out of the car my parents were at the door waiting to greet us. Dressed in matching yellow tights, long green jackets, and green pointy hats with yellow bands, Mum and Dad were certainly a sight to behold. To me, they looked like a couple of extras from a Will Ferrell Christmas movie.

"Look, Joseph," Mum said. "It's the two love birds."

As we approached, Dad outstretched his arm in readiness. "Welcome to the family, son," he said, shaking Fin's hand.

I clocked some of the neighbours at their windows, no doubt, straining to get a glimpse of Fin. Mum had obviously spread the word about her esteemed guest and alleged future son-in-law. "Sorry about this," I said to Fin, seeing that he'd noticed the audience too.

Fin leaned towards me, his voice a whisper. "I'm not worried about me anymore," he replied. "My concern is with you. Do you think you could get used to this kind of attention?"

Being honest, I didn't have a clue. As much as I couldn't deny I was tempted by Fin's desire for me to travel to America with him, it was a big decision without all the fandom that surrounded him.

Leaving the neighbours behind, we headed inside, where Vee and Mitch came out of the lounge to welcome us.

"I believe congratulations are in order," my brother-in-law said, like Dad offering Fin a celebratory handshake.

"Yes, congratulations, you two," Vee said, throwing her arms around first me and then Fin. "So have you set a date yet?"

"About that," I said, steeling myself to explain.

"Let's get those coats off you," Mum said, interrupting me before I could finish. Relieving us of our outerwear, she hung everything over the giant Santa that stood proud next to us all.

"I love that," Fin said, pointing to him.

As far as I was concerned, he was creepy.

Vee gestured she wanted a quiet word before pulling me to one side. "Thank you," she said. "For taking the heat off me." She looked down at her belly. "And this little one."

"Believe me, it's unintentional. The two of us getting married isn't even true."

My sister looked at me aghast.

"Someone heard a stupid conversation I was having with Annie and, as is usual around these parts, got it all wrong. Before I knew it Fin and I were engaged to be married, and Mum and Dad were on the phone popping corks."

Vee put a hand up to her mouth clearly trying to hide her amusement.

"It's not funny."

My sister looked over at the rest of our family. "Fin doesn't seem to mind the idea," she said.

I shook my head as he did, indeed, seem to be relishing in the misunderstanding. "That's because he's got a warped sense of humour," I said.

"You mean he's as barmy as the rest of us?" Vee replied, seeing the humour in my situation. "He's going to fit right in then, isn't he?"

I could have easily stuck my tongue out at her.

"So when are you going to tell Mum and Dad the truth?" my sister asked. "Because you seem to have given them the best Christmas present ever."

I sighed. 25th December had always been their most special day, but this year their excitement was off the chart. "As soon as I get the chance," I said.

"Come on, everyone," Mum said, rounding us all up and steering us towards the lounge. "Let's go and sit down."

I watched Fin's reaction as we entered the room, but was unable to smile at his childlike awe as he took everything in. From the stockings adorning the fireplace, to the giant tree in the corner, to the Scandinavian gnomes and yet more Santas dotted about the place, to cards hung on strings, to balloon banners to the frosted berry garlands that framed the doorways, each seemed to add to the wonder in his expression.

"I love this house," Fin said, his attention quickly turning to the curtain string lights that hung in the window.

I shook my head. In my view it was Christmas sensory overload.

Dad appeared in the doorway with a tray full of champagne glasses. "Right, everyone," he said, offering it round to us all so we could take one. "A toast."

My heart sank. I hated the fact that their elation wasn't warranted.

"This isn't fair," I said to Fin, keeping my voice low. "We need to tell them."

"It's Christmas Day, Holly," he replied, speaking equally as quiet. "Let them have their moment. We can talk about it with them later."

He was right of course. As was Vee when she said Fin and I had given my parents the best Christmas ever. Fin took hold of my hand and gave it a squeeze.

"It will all work out," he said, still keeping his voice down. "And who knows, maybe we will end up in wedded bliss."

I suddenly burst out coughing, wondering what the man was trying to do to me. In the space of just over a week we'd met, fallen in love, he'd asked me to go to America with him and suddenly he was talking about marriage. "If that was a proposal," I said, "then it's sorely lacking."

Fin let out a laugh. "I do love you, Holly Noelle."

"Are we all ready," Dad asked, raising his glass and ready to say a few words.

"Hang on a minute," Mum said. Hastening into the room, Mum took Vee's champagne glass from her, before swapping it with the mug she carried.

"I was only going to have a sip," my sister said, clearly disappointed.

"Have that instead," Mum replied. "It's raspberry leaf tea and far better for you."

As Mum turned, I saw her wink at my father, who shook his head in response.

Oh, Lordy, I thought, realising Vee had been right in her concerns. Mum was going to try and induce her into labour. "I'll take that," I said, in response. Stepping forward, I retrieved the tea from my sister. I gave her my glass, before grabbing another from the tray Dad had put to one side.

"Holly," Mum said, dismayed by my action. "We have to think of JC."

Which was exactly what I was doing.

"Mum, please don't call my baby that," Vee said. "No matter how many times you say it, I'm still not giving birth to the Second Coming."

Mum rolled her eyes. "If you're not going to drink your tea, at least let me get you some orange juice instead." She disappeared into the kitchen before returning to swap Vee's glass for a second time.

"To not just Christmas," my Dad said, at last able to finish his toast. He smiled as he looked my way. "But also to Holly and Fin."

Seeing the happiness on everyone's face's, I felt like a fraud.

"To Christmas," they all said. "And to Holly and Fin."

As everyone put their glasses to their mouths, Vee suddenly began to splutter. "What is this?" she asked, horrified.

"Like I said, fresh orange juice," Mum replied, as if wondering what the fuss was about.

I took the drink from Vee and sipped on its contents. "Undiluted orange juice, you mean. There's nothing fresh about it; it's cordial."

While Vee glared, Mum clearly feigned innocence. "I'm sorry, love. I must have picked up the wrong carton the other day when I was out shopping. They all look so similar. I forgot to take my glasses with me, you see, and as you all know, I'm blind as a bat without them."

I rolled my eyes, while Mitch clamped down on his jaw to stop himself from saying something.

"Now," Mum said, clearly knowing when to beat a hasty

retreat. "If anyone wants me, I'll be in the kitchen preparing dinner."

"Don't be adding any spices to my plate," Vee said. "I mean it."

"Would you like some help, Mary?" Fin asked, evidently trying to protect Vee and her baby as much as I was.

Halfway out the door, Mum stopped and turned. Her face lit up as bright as the Christmas tree. "You mean you and me?" she said. "Cooking Christmas lunch? Together?" Her gaze shot towards Dad. "Joseph, did you hear that?"

Dad's smile grew at the sight of Mum's obvious delight.

Mum put a hand up to her chest. "I'd be honoured to have you in my kitchen," she said.

I honestly thought the woman was about to cry.

"No, Mary," Fin replied. "*I* would be honoured."

Mum gasped. "Joseph," she said.

"Yes, love?"

"Get that camera of yours rolling. Photos, videos, I want the lot."

Fin looked my way, clearly unable to help but chuckle. I wanted the ground to swallow me whole.

36

With all of us wearing our Christmas cracker crowns, I sat in an armchair off to one side, while Vee, Mitch, Mum and Fin had squeezed onto the sofa. Dad stood in front of them, ready to take his turn at coming up with a film, book, or TV show in their somewhat rowdy game of charades.

"Are you sure you don't want to join in, Holly?" Mum asked.

"Honestly, I'm happy to just sit and watch," I replied. Not only did I have a lot on my mind, my stomach was too uncomfortable for me to partake. I'd eaten too much at Christmas lunch.

"Film!" Mum said as Dad pretended he had a movie camera up to his face.

"Three words!" Mitch joined in as Dad held three fingers up.

"Whole thing," Vee said as he used his hand to form a circle.

"*A Knight's Tale,*" Fin said as Dad began to mime.

I smiled as I watched my father try to enact whatever film he'd chosen, while the others shouted out their guesses, all of them wrong. Then again, was it any wonder, I considered, when none of Dad's actions seemed to make any sense. Observing them all together like that, it felt good to see how well Fin had slotted in, throwing himself into Christmas Day with as much gusto as was customary in the Noelle household.

My family were a funny bunch, and my smile only broadened as I looked at everyone in turn. Mum and Dad, rocking their fancy dress as if it was normal to walk around looking like a couple of elderly elves, all the while doing their best to ensure we each had a fun-filled day. Notwithstanding the fact that I'd had to intercept a handful of cod liver oil capsules when I caught Mum about to slip them into Vee's after-dinner coffee.

Vee looked as stunning as ever. Despite her complaints, pregnancy clearly suited her. She bounced up and down on the sofa, as she threw guess after guess at Dad. Goodness knew what was happening to the baby she carried; he or she was clearly being tossed around like a pancake. I chuckled, when after finding herself consistently wrong in her deductions, my sister scowled, her frustration evident. Ever since I could remember, Vee had been a sore loser.

My smile continued as I saw Mitch reach out to Vee, his accompanying expression suggesting his wife might want to refrain from jumping about quite so much and I couldn't help but giggle as Vee simply dismissed his concern in favour of winning the game. Mitch shook his head and smiled too, as if finally resigned to the fact that, pregnant or not, his wife was never going to take his advice.

My heart was full and I had to ask myself if I could really travel to America and leave those madcap, fun-loving, caring people behind.

My gaze turned to Fin, whose grin was as big as everyone else's. He must have sensed me looking at him because he glanced at me for a moment. He gave me a wink that made me feel warm and fuzzy before returning his attention to the game. Not for the first time that day, I felt torn as I watched him. Regardless of Fin's assertion that no matter what, we would work something out, could I really stay behind and risk losing the chance of true happiness? Because that's how Fin made me feel. Happy and in love and beautiful and secure... all rolled into one. But were those feelings fleeting? After all, I'd only known Fin for such a short time.

My head began to spin as my thoughts swung one way and then the other like some out-of-control pendulum. I got up from my seat and leaving everyone to their fun, headed out into the hall, telling myself I needed some fresh air.

"Where do you think you're going?" a voice said as I grabbed my coat and scarf off the giant Santa's shoulders.

I turned, smiling at Vee who'd evidently noticed I was missing and followed me out. "For a walk," I replied.

"Fancy some company?" she asked reaching for her coat. It seemed I had a walking companion whether I wanted one or not.

I shivered as we stepped outside. For once the chill in the air was just what I needed. If anything was going to help clear my befuddled brain it was a blast of wintery weather.

"Everything okay?" my sister asked, as we set off down the street.

"Of course," I replied, trying to sound upbeat. "Why do you ask?"

"Because ever since you landed you've been drifting in and out of your own little world," Vee said. "This wedding thing has really got to you, hasn't it?"

"And the rest," I replied, trying not to feel sorry for myself.

Vee laughed. "Holly, the whole town thinks you're about to marry the hottest chef on TV. What could possibly top that?"

I took a deep breath. "Can you keep a secret?"

Vee stopped still. "You mean there *is* more?"

I turned to face her. "Fin's been offered another TV project."

"That's brilliant."

I let out a laugh.

"Isn't it?" Vee asked.

"This one's in America," I said. "And Fin's asked me to go with him."

"Wow," Vee said, clearly taken aback. "That is big."

I scoffed. "Don't I know it."

My sister linked her arm in mine and we began walking again. "So are you going? And if so, when?"

"I don't know yet, but if I do it'll be soon."

"How soon?"

"He's supposed to leave on the 31st."

"Of January? But that gives you plenty of time to work things through."

I chuckled, wondering how many times I'd have to have that same conversation. "Of December."

Vee stood still for a second time, bringing me to a halt with her. "But that's only a week away. No wonder you've been away with the fairies."

"Everything just keeps running through my head. The reasons to go, the reasons to not go... I just don't know what to do, Vee."

My sister gave me a sympathetic smile as we set off down the road once more.

"Do you love Fin?"

"I feel like I do. But then I think, how can I? I've only known the man two minutes."

"Does he love you?"

My eyes lit up and butterflies whizzed around in my tummy. "He says he does."

"Then what's your problem?"

Like it was that easy. "You did hear me say the 31st of December, didn't you?"

"I've also heard you say you want some excitement and adventure. And let's face it, Fin's given you that in abundance."

Vee was right, of course. On both counts. "What if a few months away turns into a permanent thing, though? I mean who knows what this American project might lead to? How long it would be before I saw you all again?" I sighed. "And if I'm honest, I'm not sure I could cope without having my family on the doorstep. With not seeing you all regularly. The US is such a long way away."

"Not really," Vee said, matter of fact. "Thanks to technology, the world's a lot smaller than it used to be."

"And then there's the little one." I indicated my sister's belly. "It might only be weeks away, but I wouldn't be around for the birth, let alone to see him or her grow."

"Holly, it's a flight. I'm sure there'll be lots of toing and froing amongst us all."

"And what about the practicalities. I've got the house to think about and my job."

"Holly, are you even listening to what I'm saying? More to the point, are you listening to yourself?"

I realised Vee was right to pull me up. It seemed for every reason Vee gave in favour of me starting a new life with Fin, I came up with another as to why I shouldn't.

I recalled all the conversations I'd had with Mum about my cancelled trip to the Caribbean, immediately recognising the pattern. "Oh, no," I said. Bringing us both to a standstill, I looked at my sister, horrified.

"What is it?" she asked.

"I think I've turned into our mother," I replied.

37

"Where have you been?" a frantic Mitch asked. He'd obviously stood at the window looking out for Vee and me, ready to accost us as soon as we stepped through Mum and Dad's front door.

"For a walk," Vee replied, carefree as anything. "What's the problem?"

"The problem is you've been gone for hours." The man did not look happy.

"Thank goodness," Mum said as she, Dad and Fin appeared from the lounge. "We've been worried sick."

"Sorry, it's my fault," I said, understanding the concern. "We were talking and lost track of time."

"Everything okay?" Fin asked.

I nodded. "Everything's fine."

"You must be freezing, the pair of you," Mum carried on. "Get in here and warm yourselves up." She gestured towards the lounge.

Vee put her hand out to stop me from moving. "Have you made your choice?" she asked.

I nodded. "I think so."

"Good. Now if you could all go back into the living room and retake your seats," Vee said, superseding Mum. "Because Holly has something important to say, don't you?"

Fin's eyes searched mine and standing there he looked as anxious as I felt. My sister had made it abundantly clear that with her help, I'd managed to work through everything that had been running around my head and Fin knew as well as I did that what I was about to announce impacted everyone present.

Looking at everybody's anticipation, I refused to let my nerves get the better of me and instead, I steeled myself ready to tell Mum and Dad what they least wanted to hear – that Fin and I were *not* about to get married. Even more important though, was that I was about to tell the man I'd fallen deeply and madly in love with the decision I'd reached about whether I was going to America with him or not.

"What's going on?" Mum asked. "Because there'll be no *Eastenders* Christmas special in this house."

Mitch's priority stayed with his wife and unborn child. "You do know walking can induce labour, don't you?" he said to Vee.

"Can it?" Mum asked. Her soap opera fears suddenly forgotten, she looked to Dad not even trying to hide her excitement.

"Relax, Mother, it's an old wives' tale," Vee said. "Mitch is making a fuss over nothing. Walking is exercise, what harm can that–" My sister fell silent, a look of horror sweeping across her face. She dropped her head to look at the ground. "Mitch," she said, suddenly sounding like a scared little girl.

We all followed her gaze to see a pool of water at her feet.

Mitch immediately stepped forward to take command. "Battle stations, everyone. Looks like we're about to have a baby." He took his wife's hand and like a parting of the waves, the rest of us stood aside to let Mitch and Vee through. "Are you in any pain?" he asked her.

Vee shook her head. "Why? Am I supposed to be?" She sounded even more worried.

"Not necessarily," Mitch replied. "I think we're experiencing what's known as PROM. Or in layman's terms, a pre-labour rupture of the membrane. This happens in around five per cent of pregnancies so I don't want you worrying. You hear me?"

My sister nodded, for once, hanging on her husband's every word.

As was I. Concerned for Vee and the baby, as I listened to him, I, too, appreciated the reassurance.

"I'm just going to sit you on the sofa, Vee," Mitch carried on, leaving me, Fin, Mum and Dad where we were in the hall. "While I ring the hospital to let them know we're on our way."

"Joseph," Mum said. Her voice quivered as if she was struggling to contain her emotions. "This is it. Our very first grandchild."

Dad smiled, tears gathering in his eyes. "My baby's having a baby," he said, wiping them away. "I think this calls for a drink." He took a deep breath. "Fin, care to join me?"

Fin looked my way as if needing my approval and finding such a response both respectful and sweet, I smiled and nodded, encouraging him to go for it.

"You go too," Mum said, at the same time looking down at Vee's puddle. "I'll get the mop."

While she headed off for her cleaning apparatus, I did as I was told and followed Dad and Fin into the lounge. Mitch conversed on his phone with the hospital's maternity staff while Dad headed straight for the whisky bottle.

"Don't mind me," Vee said, watching Dad pour himself and Fin a drink. "I'm only in bloody labour." She turned to me. "I see he's not offering you one either."

"Right," Mitch said, stuffing his mobile into his pocket. "Time for us to go."

"We'll give you head start," I said, my excitement building. "Then follow on. That's if you don't mind us being there?"

"It might mean you're at the hospital for a while," Mitch said. "Possibly all night."

"That's okay," I replied. "It's not as if we have anything more important on."

"Have you got your hospital bag?" Mum asked, charging into the room.

"All ready and waiting in the car," Mitch replied.

"And has been for the last three months," Vee said. She let Mitch help her onto her feet. "My husband hasn't left anything to chance."

"Come here, love," Dad said, pulling his youngest daughter into a hug.

"I'll go and start the car," Mitch said.

As he headed out, I felt guilty for all the times I'd secretly mocked my brother-in-law's pregnancy reading. Having watched him put some of what he'd learnt into action, it was clear the man deserved nothing but respect.

Mum took Dad's place, wrapping her arms tight around Vee's shoulders. "Thank you," she said. "I thought these two had made my Christmas." Mum indicated Fin and me. "But to have a Christmas baby..." Her words faltered as her emotions again took over.

"Oh, Mum, please," my sister said, coming over all weepy too. "You're setting me off now."

As Mum stepped away from Vee, I stepped forward. "It's a big thank you from me too," I said, throwing my arms around my sister. "For listening. Now go on. Go welcome this baby of yours into the world."

"Not so fast," Vee said, glancing over at Fin. "Well, come on. You may as well give the pregnant lady a hug too."

He smiled, appearing more than happy to comply. Although

as he leaned in, I saw a seriousness appear on his face as Vee whispered something in his ear. He nodded in response, while I wondered what words of wisdom had been exchanged.

"You ready?" Mitch asked, reappearing from outside.

"For what I'm about to go through?" Vee asked. "As I'll ever be, I suppose."

38

We all followed my sister and brother-in-law out into the hall, but while Fin and I saw them off from the doorstep, Mum and Dad went out to the car. They fussed around the parents-to-be, making sure seat belts were buckled and promises to drive safely were given. And when Vee and Mitch, at last, drove off, the two of them stood there until the vehicle was nowhere to be seen.

"You okay?" Fin asked.

I smiled as I watched my madcap parents in their elf outfits embrace each other. They'd spent months eagerly awaiting the arrival of their first grandchild and now the time was almost upon them, they appeared a little overwhelmed. "I can't believe in the next few hours my little sister will have had a baby." I felt Fin's arm reach around my shoulders. "I'm glad you're here," I said.

He kissed the top of my head. "Me too."

"Well this is exciting, isn't it?" Mum said as she and Dad made their return.

We all stood there in silence staring into the distance as if my sister's car was still in full view. It seemed we all needed a minute to absorb what was happening.

"Time to put the kettle on," Mum suddenly said, at the same time ushering us all back inside.

"But don't you want to get going?" I asked, surprised to hear otherwise.

"To the hospital?" Mum replied. She laughed as if I'd said something stupid.

"We've got hours yet," Dad said. "There's no rush."

"And we're going to need to load ourselves up on caffeine if we're to get through the night," Mum said. "Besides, I thought you had some announcement to make?"

In all the excitement I'd managed to forget about that. "It's nothing, really," I said, trying to delay the inevitable. "It can wait."

"Rubbish," Mum said. "You three go and sit yourselves down. The drinks will be ready in no time."

As me, Fin and Dad filed back into the lounge, I took a deep breath, feeling my pulse race as I anticipated everyone's response. Dad headed for the sofa, while Fin and I sat in an armchair each. I could see Fin was nervous. Like everyone else, he hadn't a clue what I was about to say. I hadn't even told Vee what decision I'd come to and she was the one I'd discussed everything with.

True to her word, Mum joined us minutes later with a tray of coffee cups. "There's sugar here if you need it, Fin," she said, handing out the drinks. She perched on the sofa next to Dad. "Now what was it you wanted to say, Holly?"

All eyes on me, I wasn't sure where to begin. I told myself I may as well start with the wedding debacle and the fact that there wasn't going to be one. "Well. The thing is..."

"I have to go back to the US," Fin said, interrupting me mid-sentence. "To start another work project."

I flashed him a look wondering what he was doing.

"Ooh, that sounds exciting," Mum said. "For the telly?"

Fin nodded. "It is, yes."

"Are we allowed to know what it entails?" Mum asked, clearly keen to know more.

Dad leaned forward in his seat. "In America, you say?" he said, sticking to the salient point.

Fin nodded.

"So when do you have to leave?" Dad said.

Here we go, I thought.

"On the 31st," Fin said.

"Of January?" Dad said.

"December."

Mum appeared mortified. "But what about the wedding? How can you plan a wedding if you're in two different countries?"

"About that," I said, ready to explain there was never going to be any wedding for a second time.

"I've asked Holly..." Fin looked at me nervously, "...to come with me."

Mum and Dad stared at him aghast. "But you leave in a week," they both said.

"I do," he replied.

"And *are* you going with him?" Dad asked me.

Fin shifted to the edge of his seat, evidently wanting to know the answer to that question too.

I looked at Fin direct. "Yes."

"You are?" Fin asked, appearing both surprised and relieved.

"You are?" Mum and Dad said.

I smiled at Fin. "I am."

"Fantastic." Fin couldn't seem to stop grinning, his gaze not leaving mine.

"That is good news," Dad said.

"It certainly is," Mum said.

"Excuse me?" Frowning in confusion, I immediately turned my attention to my parents. "Are you for real?" I thought about my Caribbean holiday and the response it had received. While Dad might have understood the reasons behind it, Mum hadn't at all. The guilt trip I'd been put through every time I spoke to her had been unbearable. After the way she'd gone on, I'd expected at least some dissent on her part.

"Like you keep saying," Mum said. "You need some excitement and adventure in your life."

"Not too much adventure, mind," Dad said, looking at Fin. "We all know what some of these TV people are like."

"Don't worry, Holly's safe with me," Fin said.

"So is that where you'll be getting married?" Mum asked. "In America." She turned to Dad, giving him a quick tap on the knee. "We've never been to America, have we?"

I yet again opened my mouth to tell my parents the truth about that to find myself yet again prevented.

"We haven't decided yet," Fin said.

"We haven't?" I asked, wondering what the man was talking about.

"To be honest, Holly hasn't really agreed to marry me yet."

"But I thought..." Mum turned her attention to me. "Why not?" she asked.

Fin had a glint in his eye as he also looked my way. "As marriage proposals go, apparently mine was sorely lacking."

I almost laughed as I remembered our conversation that morning. Fin had either taken my words out of context or I'd been one hundred per cent right.

I swallowed hard as I watched Fin get up from his seat and walk towards me. He transfixed me with his gaze as he got down on one knee. "*What is he doing?*" I thought to myself. Fin's behaviour was not in the script I'd mentally prepared.

216

"Holly Noelle," Fin said. "I fell in love with you the moment I saw you." He smiled. "Even with all that mascara smudged down your face."

I heard Mum gasp. "Joe, look. He's proposing. Again."

"And while you probably won't believe me," Fin continued. "I knew there and then that I wanted to spend the rest of my life with you." He took my hands. "Which is why, Holly Noelle, I'm asking you to marry me?"

Tears welled in my eyes and my heart raced as I let out a nervous giggle. Feeling like all my Christmases had come at once, I wondered if I was dreaming.

Fin willed me to say something.

"Yes," I said, by then in danger of snivelling. "I will marry you."

I heard Mum squeal in delight as Fin stood up to pull me out of the chair and onto my feet. "Are you sure about this?" he asked, keeping his voice low.

"I'm sure," I said, whispering back.

He leaned down to give me a long lingering kiss and forgetting all about my parents for a moment I melted in his arms.

"This calls for another drink," Dad said, interrupting the moment.

I giggled again as Fin and I, at last, separated.

"I love you, Holly Noelle," Fin said.

"I love you too, Finlay McCormack."

"Care to join me, Fin?" Dad asked.

"Thank you, Joseph," he replied. "I think I will."

"Oh, come here, you two," Mum said. Jumping up from her seat, she threw her arms around us in a wonderful trio hug. "This really is the best Christmas ever."

Accepting Mum's embrace, I couldn't agree more.

39

NEW YEAR'S EVE

It had been a busy few days getting ready for our departure to the US. I'd packed and re-packed my suitcase over and over again, feeling sure I'd left something important out on each occasion. I'd had to hand my notice in at work, not that I'd been able to give any. Ruth, my manager, had been great about that. She'd said, "I don't suppose you'll need it, Holly, but if you ever do, there'll always be a job for you at the bookshop."

The worst part of leaving had been saying goodbye to Annie. As expected, we both cried buckets and while she threatened Fin with bodily harm if he failed to look after me, I sought assurances from Emma and Josh that they would look after Annie in return. Me and my friend agreed to video call at least once a month to update each other on wedding plans and grandchild news. To say I was going to miss that woman was an understatement.

Sitting with Fin in the airport café, I couldn't believe how quickly the time to leave had come around. I was about to start a whole new chapter in life, a step that felt both exciting and challenging at the same time.

"Are you okay?" Fin asked. Reaching over to take my hand, he obviously saw I was nervous.

I looked at my watch. "I'm just wondering where they've all got to," I said, checking the doors for the gazillionth time.

"They'll be here," Fin said, demonstrating a tad more confidence than me.

"It would be just like them to miss a turning and end up at the wrong terminal," I said, wondering why Mum, Dad, Vee and Mitch hadn't arrived yet. The thought of boarding the plane without seeing them was enough to bring a lump to my throat. "I knew we should have said our goodbyes last night."

Fin gazed at me, concerned. "I know you're going to miss them. You have a wonderful family and if I were in your shoes I'd feel the same." He chuckled. "In fact, strike that. I do feel the same. I might have only met them a week ago, but they've certainly made an impression."

I let out a laugh, thinking about how eccentric we all were. "We Noelles have a habit of doing that."

"But you are looking forward to this, aren't you? You don't have any regrets about coming with me?"

I looked back at Fin, mortified that he might think such a thing. "Of course I don't have any regrets. The fact that you wanted me to come might have been a shock to the system, but now... I love you, Fin. It's as simple as that. And where you go, I go."

Fin smiled at me, his eyes full of the intensity I'd grown used to. He squeezed my fingers. "I love you too."

"There they are!" I heard Dad's voice say. "I hope we haven't cut it too fine."

I jumped to my feet and turned, relieved to see not just him, but the rest of the Noelles in tow. Mum and Dad, wearing matching jumpers. Her with a box of tissues at the ready. Him, with a great big smile on his face. Vee and Mitch, looking very much the proud parents of baby Angelica who lay fast asleep in her carrier.

They hadn't even reached our table and I could see Mum was already crying. "Don't worry," she said, between snivels. "These are tears of joy."

"Really?" I asked.

Mum threw her arms around me. "I'm sad for myself, but so, so happy for you."

I hugged her tight, a part of me never wanting to let the woman go.

"You can blame this little one for us being late," Vee said, gesturing to baby Angelica as me and Mum finally released each other. "Halfway along the motorway she decided to bring her breakfast up."

I peered into her carrier. Fast asleep, the little one certainly lived up to her name, looking like the little angel she was. I smiled, unable to help but wonder why Vee would carry on the tradition of giving Christmassy names to the Noelle offspring. When explaining, my sister simply said she couldn't help herself. Although she'd been adamant that if she'd given birth to a boy, no way would she have called her son *Jesus* like our mother had hoped. I reached into the carrier and stroked Angelica's perfect pudding face, knowing that the next time I saw her I might not recognise her.

"We had to stop off at the services to sort her out," Vee said, looking down at her daughter with me.

"My turn now," Dad said. He stepped forward to embrace me, while Mum moved on to Fin. "Promise me one thing," Dad said, squeezing me with all his might.

"Anything," I replied.

He pulled back. "While you're off on this adventure, you make time to follow that dream of yours and write that novel."

"I will," I said. "I promise."

"And you, lad," Dad said to Fin, turning to hug him with the same sincerity. "Make sure you take care of this daughter of mine."

"You can count on it," Fin replied.

"I'm really going to miss you," Vee said.

"And vice versa," I replied. "If we're still in the US when Angelica is big enough to travel all that way, I expect you to come and stay."

Vee laughed. "Just you try to stop us."

My emotions started to get the better of me. "And please send lots of photos." I looked at my niece again, still fast asleep, and completely unaware of the blubbing farewells going on around her. "And videos," I added. "She might not be doing much now, but that won't last long and I don't want to miss anything."

Tears welled in Vee's eyes and she turned away as if trying to protect me from them.

"I can't wait to hear about this new life you're embarking on, Holly," Mitch said, taking my sister's place.

I threw my arms around him. "I'll keep you updated."

"Looks like it's time to go, Holly," Fin said, checking his watch.

Another round of hugs took place amongst all of us, neither the leaving nor the staying party wanting them to end.

"To think, the next time we'll all be together it will probably be your wedding," Mum said, handing round yet more tissues.

"I'm going to miss you all so much," I said, burning the sight of each and every one of them into my memory.

"You'll be too busy having fun," Dad said. "Now go on, you don't want to miss that flight."

"Ready?" Fin asked.

I took a deep breath. "Ready."

I gave everyone one last hug and a kiss, before grabbing my

suitcase with one hand, and Fin's palm with the other. I took a deep breath as we began heading for security and the departure lounge beyond. Refusing to look back, my eyes welled again and tears started to fall.

"Let us know you get there all right!" Mum said.

"Say hello to George Clooney for me," Vee said, a statement that broke through my upset to make me chuckle.

"Do no such thing," Mitch said, making me laugh a little more.

"Most of all, follow that dream," Dad called out.

"You ready?" Fin asked, lifting my hand and kissing it as we reached the door that left my life in the UK behind.

Fin and I grinned at each other and taking a deep breath in readiness, we stepped through to the other side, ready to start our new life together.

THE END

ACKNOWLEDGEMENTS

Well what a year it's been. It's just like us to move to a new country and start a house hunt the week before lockdown began. Finding ourselves homeless and living in a campervan for six months was certainly an experience, although throughout that experience we met some wonderful people. From the lovely chap who offered to re-charge our van battery and wash our clothes when we were parked up at the beach. To the council worker who asked his bosses to delay closing that beach until the next day just so he could give us fair warning. To the chap in the garage who happily kept charging my laptop up for me so I could keep on writing... I don't know your names, but your acts of kindness will always be remembered.

I'd particularly like to thank Siubhán and Ciaran at Corcreggan Mill. I'm not sure I'd have been able to write this book if you two hadn't given us a place to stay when Covid restrictions really kicked in. You provided Robert and me, two people whom you'd never even met, with a sense of security during a very strange time and when we did finally get to meet you both in person, you were every bit as lovely as we'd imagined. As for your three little girls... They certainly know how to throw a tea party!

Another Corcreggan mention goes to Conal. As soon as you happened to mention that you cook for a living, I inundated you with questions about what life is like in a professional kitchen. Of course, when I then asked you to jot it all down you must have thought *who is this woman?* But jot it down you did. Thank you. I hope I've done your notes justice.

I'd like to thank Cheryl Phoenix and Federica Angelè for answering what must have seemed like silly questions. Holly attempting to check in for her flight might not take up much of the story but the devil is in the detail as they say. I appreciate you giving me your time and especially your patience as I tried, rather clumsily, to relay what information I needed. Thank you, ladies.

What can I say about my Facebook and Twitter followers? You certainly came to my aid when I put out a call for potential names for Fin's cookery show. Your suggestions weren't just fun they were inspired! Thanks to Natalie Johnson for coming up with 'Cooking Hell' and Blue Poppy Publishing for taking this one step further with your catch phrases. I'm still giggling.

Of course, my appreciation goes out to everyone at Bloodhound Books. Betsy, Fred, Tara, Clare, Shirley, Heather, the publicity team and my cover designer... You're a great team to work with and as always, I'm thankful for your support. I'm especially grateful for the extra work you've all put in to bring this book out in time for Christmas. You are all absolute stars.

Finally, I'd like to thank all my readers, without whom I wouldn't be doing the job I love. I hope my stories continue to make you laugh and, at times, cry. And enable you to escape to the same happy place they take me as I write them.

Stay safe, everyone, and here's to a very merry Christmas for all of us.

Suzie x

Lightning Source UK Ltd.
Milton Keynes UK
UKHW012012221120
373896UK00002B/74